BY KIM MEDINA

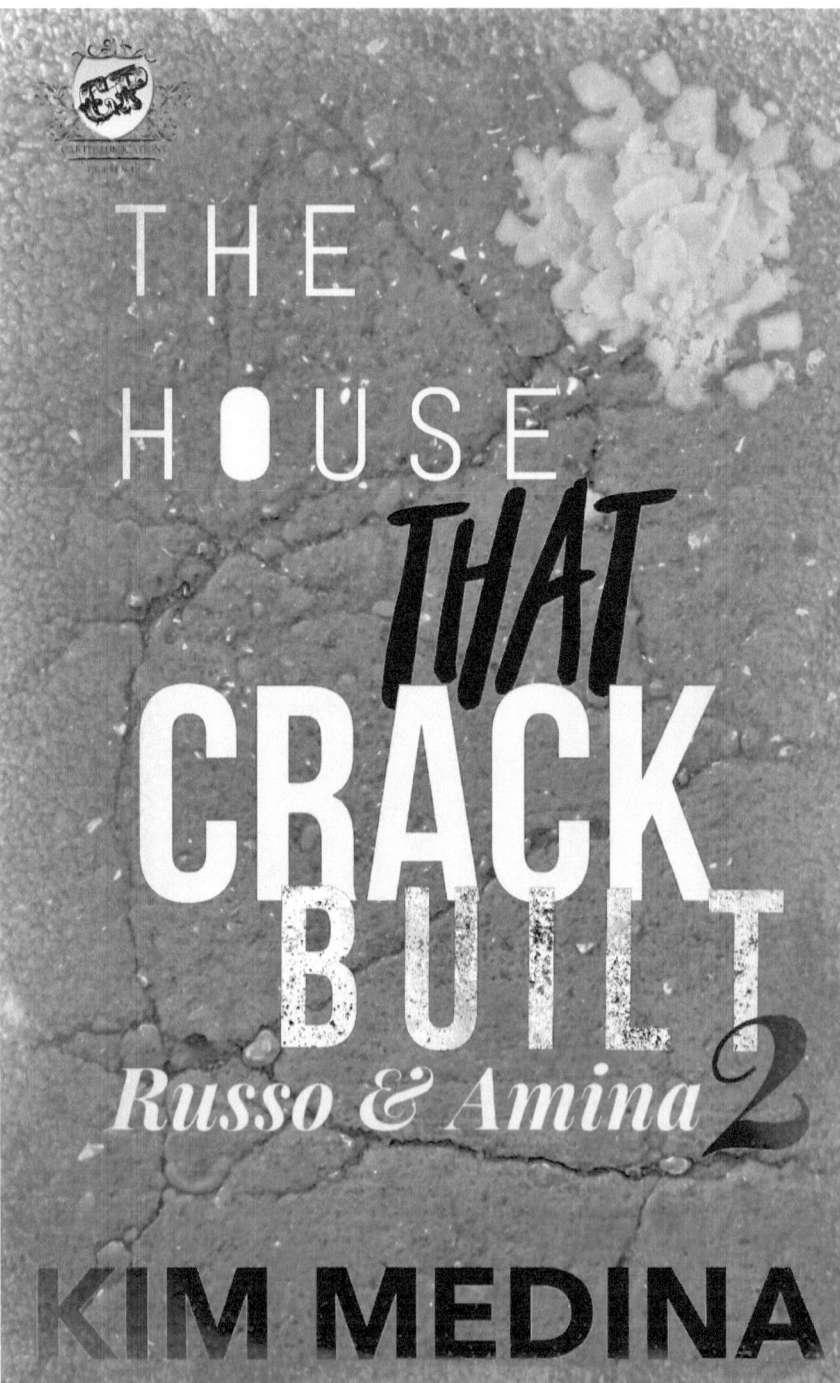

THE HOUSE THAT CRACK BUILT

Russo & Amina 2

KIM MEDINA

THE HOUSE THAT CRACK BUILT 2

ARE YOU ON OUR EMAIL
LIST?

SIGN UP ON OUR WEBSITE

www.thecartelpublications.com

OR TEXT THE WORD:

CARTELBOOKS TO 22828

FOR PRIZES, CONTESTS, ETC.

4

CHECK OUT OTHER TITLES BY THE CARTEL PUBLICATIONS

THE HOUSE THAT CRACK BUILT 2

Pretty Kings 4: Race's Rage
Hersband Material
Upscale Kittens
Wake & Bake Boys
Young & Dumb
Young & Dumb: Vyce's Getback
Tranny 911
Tranny 911: Dixie's Rise
First Comes Love, Then Comes Murder
Luxury Tax
The Lying King
Crazy Kind of Love
Silence of The Nine
Silence of The Nine II: Let There Be Blood
Prison Throne
Goon
Hoetic Justice
And They Call Me God
The Ungrateful Bastards
Lipstick Dom
A School of Dolls
Skeezers
Skeezers 2
You Kissed Me Now I Own You
Nefarious
Redbone 3: The Rise Of The Fold
The Fold
Clown Niggas
The One You Shouldn't Trust
Cold As Ice
The Whore The Wind Blew My Way
She Brings The Worst Kind
The House That Crack Built
The House That Crack Built 2
The End. How To Write A Bestselling Novel in 30 Days

WWW.THECARTELPUBLICATIONS.COM

THE HOUSE THAT CRACK BUILT 2:

Russo & Amina

BY

KIM MEDINA

Library of Congress Control Number: 2017955523

ISBN 10: 194524089X

ISBN 13: 978-1945240898

Cover Design: Cover Design: Bookslutgirl.com

www.thecartelpublications.com
First Edition
Printed in the United States of America

What's Up Fam,

Happy Holidays! It's that time of the year again. I personally love the holiday's man. To me it's nothing like decorating the house and sitting back with something cold, or hot ;) while listening to Christmas music and marveling at the lights. It's one of the best feelings in the world. Just being grateful and counting blessings. I truly cherish it and I wish nothing but happiness for you and your family!

Now, right down to business... "The House That Crack Built 2"! This novel is fire!! I didn't think Kim could do it again, but I must admit, this one is better than the first! If you loved how part one shocked you, taught you and gave you a good story, then I know you'll be here for part 2!

With that being said, keeping in line with tradition, we want to give respect to a vet or trailblazer paving the way. In this novel, we would like to recognize:

RICKEY SMILEY

THE HOUSE THAT CRACK BUILT 2

Broderick "Rickey" Smiley is an American Stand Up Comedian turned Actor, TV host, On Air Personality and most recently, Author. He's penned his memoir entitled, *Stand By Your Truth: And Then Run For Your Life*". This novel is a mash-up of life lessons, a testimonial and standing in truth all through a comedic voice. Make sure you show Rickey some love and check it out!

Aight, get to it. I'll catch you in the next book.

Be Easy!

Charisse "C. Wash" Washington
Vice President
The Cartel Publications
www.thecartelpublications.com
www.facebook.com/publishercwash
Instagram: publishercwash
www.twitter.com/cartelbooks
www.facebook.com/cartelpublications
Follow us on Instagram: Cartelpublications
#CartelPublications
#UrbanFiction

#PrayForCeCe

#RickeySmiley

CARTEL URBAN CINEMA'S 3rd WEB SERIES

BMORE CHICKS
@ **Pink Crystal Inn**

NOW AVAILABLE:

Via

YOUTUBE

And

DVD

(Season 2 Coming in January)

www.youtube.com/user/tstyles74

www.cartelurbancinema.com

www.thecartelpublications.com

CARTEL URBAN CINEMA's **2nd** MOVIE

MOTHER MONSTER

The movie based off the book,

"RAUNCHY"

by

T. Styles

Now Available on You Tube

Available to Download via VIMEO

www.cartelurbancinema.com and

www.thecartelpublications.com

CARTEL URBAN CINEMA'S 2nd WEB SERIES

IT'LL COST YOU (Twisted Tales Season One)

NOW AVAILABLE:
YOUTUBE / STREAMING / DVD

www.youtube.com/user/tstyles74

www.cartelurbancinema.com

www.thecartelpublications.com

CARTEL URBAN CINEMA'S 1st WEB SERIES

THE WORST OF US (Season One & Season Two)

NOW AVAILABLE:

YOUTUBE / STREAMING/ DVD

www.youtube.com/user/tstyles74

www.cartelurbancinema.com

www.thecartelpublications.com

THE HOUSE THAT CRACK BUILT 2

CARTEL URBAN CINEMA'S 1st MOVIE

PITBULLS IN A SKIRT – THE MOVIE

www.cartelurbancinema.com and

www.amazon.com

www.thecartelpublications.com

#TheHouseThatCrackBuilt2

‘

The problem with lies is this...they're greedy and
need more frequent and bigger lies to survive.
And that's when they destroy.

PROLOGUE

*R*ain poured heavily down on Baltimore City as thunder clapped against the sky overhead. Most of the city's residents chose to stay hidden within the walls of their homes but Amina didn't have the luxury because she was being hunted for dear life by her husband Russo.

"Please leave me alone!" She yelled as she continued to bolt as fast as she could. One of her shoes had fallen off some ways back, which meant her bare toes pressed against broken vials and filth as she dipped in and out of dark alleyways.

But Russo wouldn't give up his chase. Armed with a silver .45 he made it evident that he had one mission, to put his princess out of her misery.

Forever.

When Amina looked back, she tripped over a brick in front of her, causing her to break her big toe. Hysterical, when she rolled on her back, the rain continuing to smack at her face, Russo came into view.

With outstretched hands she begged for her life. "Please don't do this to me. I love you."

THE HOUSE THAT CRACK BUILT 2

He smiled at her sinisterly, cocked his weapon and....BOOM!

CHAPTER ONE

TWO MONTHS EARLIER

AMINA

We had so much to do in preparation for Reggie's mother's party. And although I was exhausted because Tamika let my four-year-old daughter Naverly, watch a scary movie with her yesterday, which meant she was up with me all night in my bed, I was excited for him. Gina had two years clean off of drugs and Reggie couldn't stop the blushing that would show up on his face every time he talked about her.

We rented ten tables and decorated them all in purple and black, Gina's favorite colors due to her love for the Baltimore Ravens. I just finished placing down the last tablecloth when I looked over at Tamika because I called her several times with no answer. She seemed as if she was in her mind and I was worried.

"Everything cool?" I asked. She continued to daydream. I walked over, grabbed her hand and said, "Tamika, are you okay?"

She smiled. "Uh...yeah. Why you say that?"

I sat down and she sat down too. "Then why it seem like you ain't? Lately you seem like you here but not really. Now stop playing around and talk to me."

"I don't know." She shrugged. "At one point I was thinking about Drillo and the next...Gina was on my mind."

I took a deep breath. "Okay, first things first." I cleared my throat. "I thought we came to an understanding with Drillo."

"We did."

"So what's the problem now?"

"Mama." She said seriously. "Mama made us promise to stay together and what we do? Abandon him when he needed us the most. It's so wrong."

I took another deep breath. "Tamika, I know we promised to stick together but we can't have Drillo in our home right now. First we got Naverly who is real impressionable and then with all of us in college, it'll be too much to support him when he really doesn't want our help."

She lowered her gaze and looked away from me. "So we abandon him? When he really needs us?"

"Come on now, Tamika. You know that's not the case."

"Then how is it?" Her chin quivered. "Because it looks an awful like we're abandoning him to me."

"You act like we don't fake leave money on the table every night so he can take it. You act like we haven't spent thousands of dollars in new doors and windows because instead of knocking and asking for help he'd rather steal from us and break inside."

"Amina, don't—"

"Don't what?" I yelled as tears started to roll down my face.

I didn't want to have this conversation for more reasons than one. For starters I felt guilty deep down because we couldn't do more for Drillo. And because part of me felt like I had chosen my daughter and husband over him.

"All I want to do is fight for us right now." I paused. "Besides, we tried time and time again to get Drillo some help and each time he refused. Now you making me feel like I should keep trying, even if it means dragging us down too."

Tamika looked at me and pulled me into a hug. "I'm sorry for upsetting you."

THE HOUSE THAT CRACK BUILT 2

I took a deep breath. "I know you didn't mean to. You were just speaking your mind like you should."

She separated from me. "I think I'm really mad about something else too and I don't know how to say it." She looked behind her at the door and back at me.

"What is it about? Just get it off your chest."

"Gina. She's—"

"Is it party time yet?" Reggie yelled walking into the backyard with a ton of purple and black balloons and a smile on his face. "'Cause it's a celebration!"

I wiped the tears off my face quickly and walked over to him to take the balloons. Reggie had been standing true to his promise to my mother to look after us and the last thing I needed was him thinking I was upset.

After sitting the balloons on the table that held the food I watched him walk up to my sister, grip her in a hug and kiss her softly on the lips. They loved each other like crazy and I still couldn't believe our lives had turned out so amazing.

But once again, I knew ugliness was coming our way too.

Seconds later Russo came through the door with Naverly on his shoulders. Both of them were smiling and I took a few seconds to stare at them with all the love welling up in my heart. Today she was dressed just like her dad. They were both wearing white t-shirts with gold chains, jeans and purple and black Nike Foams.

I walked over to him, kissed him deeply and grabbed Naverly. Her curly hair was in two pigtails and she smelled like baby lotion. That's one thing I kept was my daughter fresh in all meanings of the word.

When I looked at Russo harder I saw a red lipstick print on his face. Suddenly I felt gut punched. I took my thumb, rubbed it off and asked. "Fuck is this?"

Reggie and Tamika looked at us too, probably hearing the anger in my voice.

And then Russo looked at Reggie and they both broke out into laughter. "Fuck is funny?"

"That's Mrs. Connelly," Reggie said. "We helped her with her groceries before we got here. You know how she is. Always kissing niggas on the face and shit."

I felt like the air was pressed from my lungs. "Why would you think I would step out on you?"

THE HOUSE THAT CRACK BUILT 2

He said playfully. "I'm the happiest I've ever been in my life. Never think of me that way. I'm not in the business of hurting my wife and that ain't never changing."

"I'm sorry." I lowered my head and he pushed my chin up lightly so that I was looking into his eyes.

"My wife ain't got shit to be sorry for. Believe that."

"So ya'll wanna hear what I got my moms?" Reggie asked. He was smiling wide.

I turned and looked toward him. Real excitedly he said, "I paid the taxes off on that house and I'm gonna sell it."

We all looked across the yard at the dilapidated house directly on the other side of ours. "Congratulations!" I said. "You can finally put that chapter behind you."

"With the money I'm gonna buy my mother her own house. So she can start over."

"I told you, I can give you the money now, man." Russo said. "Ain't no big deal."

"Nah, Yo, you already put me on." He paused. "I wanna do this myself. Plus I like spending time with both of my girls in here while it lasts." He looked at Tamika and pulled her into a one-arm embrace before kissing her lips. "I'ma do this my way."

"Respect." Russo said.

"So what time she gonna get here?" Tamika asked Reggie.

He looked at his silver Apple watch. "She said about 8:00. That gives us a few hours to put the finishing touches on things."

I looked at Tamika again who didn't seem too enthused. And I wondered what was she going to tell me before they came home.

CHAPTER TWO

GINA

*G*ina rolled over on a dirty mattress that sat on the floor of a dope house. Her temples throbbed as she rubbed them, trying to reduce the pain. When she opened her eyes she looked at the dirty yellow ceiling, which held bubbled paint, and roach clubs that nested in the corners.

Sitting up straight, she looked upon the five or six sleeping strangers she didn't recognize. How did she get here? Why wasn't she in the safety of her home with her son?

Immediately she was bombarded with memories of what happened the night before. After almost two years of being off drugs, she met up with an old flame and gave up her sobriety.

"Hey sexy," a groggy voice said from the corner.

When she looked toward the area she saw Frank, smiling at her, as he sat on the floor his upper body leaning against the wall. "What a night right?"

"I can't believe this happened." She rubbed her head and looked down at herself. With the exception of her bra and panties she was wearing

nothing. "My son is going to be so disappointed and he'll have every right too."

He crawled toward her, sat on the bed and gripped her into his arms. His pits smelling of raw onions and dirt. "If he loves you then he'll understand."

"But what if he doesn't forgive me?" Her voice cracked and her heart thumped wildly. "I don't...I don't think I'll ever be able to forgive myself."

"What's so bad about what we do anyway?" He paused. "Huh? Because I'm confused."

She frowned and looked around the dump they were sitting in. "You mean what's wrong besides everything? Look at us, Frank. We a mess right now."

"Gina, we didn't ask to have this life now did we? It happened to us and now we have to deal with it the best way we know how. And if people in our lives don't—"

"You don't understand, Frank! My son wanted me back in his life. Despite everything I did to him when I left him in that house he wanted me back and look...I...I can't even keep a promise to stay clean."

"I get all that but I have one question for you." He smiled. "Do you wanna think about our troubles or you wanna get high again? Because I don't know 'bout you but I wanna feel good. Later for all this other shit."

Her eyebrows raised and her mouth watered at the thought. "I...I wanna..."

"Say no more!" Frank leapt up. "I'm gonna find a mark. You stay right here."

She looked up at him. "I don't know about doing that again because—"

"You still love me, G? Please say you do because I still love you." He paused. "And unlike your son I need you."

"Of course I love you. That has never changed. But I...I wanted to be better than this. I wanted to do better."

He frowned. "Well what about me? You broke my heart when you left me to move back with your son. A son who has his own life and a new wife. You think he gonna let you stay with him forever? Huh?" As he yelled spit flew from his lips and smacked against her face. "Nah! What he gonna do is put you out the moment he gets a chance." He kneeled down to look into her eyes. "But I could never do that to you because I love you too much."

She nodded, tears rolling down her cheeks. "I know you do and I know you're right."

"Then stay right here." He stood up again. *"I'll be right back."*

When he left she closed her eyes tightly and took a deep breath. *"God, I know I don't deserve much. I know I'm not worthy of Your love and attention but I'm begging you to give me a sign that this is not what I should be doing. Give me a sign that is clear so that I will know that it came from you, specifically for me. I'm begging."*

"That's my bed!" A junkie yelled having rolled over only to see Gina sitting on it with her eyes closed.

She opened her lids. *"Excuse me?"*

"You sitting on my bed, bitch! Get off!" She paused. *"You don't belong here! GET OUT! GET OUT!"*

Gina was so enraged she rushed over to the woman and kicked her in the stomach, sending her running out the door yelling obscenities the entire way. She was so caught up in her emotions she didn't understand that when God answers prayers, he uses even the wicked and the angry to get his point across.

Out of breath she sat back on the bed, looked around and hated everything she saw. *"I asked for help and this is how you repay me?"* She yelled at

THE HOUSE THAT CRACK BUILT 2

Him. *"You never cared about me! You only cared about the pain you were putting me in!"* She continued yelling at God.

"Who you talking to, bae?" Frank said entering the room.

"Uh...nobody."

He sat next to her. *"Good, because I need you on your best."* He looked down at her and removed her bra, allowing her 'A' cups to go free. *"I told him he gotta pay no less than forty dollars."* He rubbed his hands together greedily.

She backed up a little. *"Where you find him?"*

He stuffed his fingers into her panties and sniffed. *"Damn, you a little dank."* He said as if he could talk. He crawled over to where she was, grabbed a dry rag and handed it to her. *"Wipe some of the juice off. It's fishy."*

She removed her panties and wiped her foul smelling juices away as best she could without water. *"Who is he?"*

"Don't worry 'bout all that." He smiled. *"Just know that I'll never forget what you doing for me. And for us."* He placed his dry hand on the side of her face. *"Nobody has ever been there for me on a regular basis. My kids left me and even my wife*

when I fell on hard times but I always knew you would come back. And I was right too."

She nodded, and tried to keep the thought of her son out of her mind. "I love you."

"I know you do." When she looked down he raised her chin. "That's why nothing or no one is going to keep us apart."

"IS FRANK HERE!" A man called from the other room as he walked into the house.

"Good, now he here," he whispered. "I need you to suck him first to get him hard and then give him the best pussy you ever did in your life."

"So I'm fucking him and sucking him for only forty?"

"You doing it as a favor to me."

"But that's not enough of—"

"So you abandoning me again?"

"No...I...of course not."

"Then stop wasting time and do what you gotta do."

The man came into the room and she recognized him immediately. His name was Pigs. It had been rumored that he had herpes but since he paid the women in the dope house so often to top him off, most overlooked his shortcomings. He walked up to her, weighing three hundred pounds

THE HOUSE THAT CRACK BUILT 2

easily. He smiled when he saw her because Gina had been loved on for two years straight, which meant the cloak most dope heads wore from being in the streets hadn't surrounded her yet.

He unzipped his pants, walked up to her and said, "Open wide."

She looked at Frank. "Do it, baby." He kissed her on the cheek. "I love you so much."

She smiled, looked up at the John and gave him the best dome of his life.

CHAPTER THREE
RUSSO

When I pulled up to my wife's house I went off when I saw the bum nigga from down the block on the lawn. I had to run him off at least five times already and whenever I brought it up to Amina, she was dead set on staying in that piece of shit she called a home. Why we gotta live here when I got a perfectly good crib with enough rooms where we ain't ever got to see each other again if we don't want to.

I parked, got out and ran up to him. "Scram, nigga!"

"I was just—"

"I don't give a fuck what you was 'bout to do. Fuck from 'round my wife's house with this shit."

It wasn't until he turned around that I saw he had his dick out. I was about to splatter his brains on the side of the house when Mrs. Connelly came out and yelled, "Don't, Russo!"

Wow. Her timing was legendary.

I looked back at her and took a deep breath before focusing on the dude. "I'm not gonna say

THE HOUSE THAT CRACK BUILT 2

shit else. You got five seconds to get invisible. Not a second more."

He took off running and I opened the door to the house. My baby girl was on the floor playing with a puzzle and I saw Amina in the kitchen. I kissed my kid and rushed up to wifey.

"Do you know that bum ass nigga was out front again?" I pointed toward the door.

She waved her hand at me. "Stop trying to look for reasons to fight. We not moving so don't ask me again."

"That's what you think I get off on?" I asked, my nostrils flaring. "Fighting you?"

"All I'm saying is that we need to keep the drama down to a minimum. With Gina not coming home last night for that party, Reggie been in a bad mood."

"I get all that." I said, my voice deepening. "And I'ma look after my man later. But right now I wanna know when you gonna move to my crib?" I pointed at the floor. "'Cause I ain't feeling my daughter being up in here. And it ain't like you don't know that already."

She took a deep breath, turned around and crossed her arms over her chest. If she wasn't so sexy I'd be just as mad, but with her hair in a bun and her nipples poking out of that white top she was wearing, for real all I thought about was bending her over that sink and...well...that ain't what's on my mind now.

"Russo, we talked about this shit already. I'm not about to move my daughter in that house with you being a...uh..." she cleared her throat and I moved closer.

"What you was 'bout to say?" I took one step closer. "Let me hear the words."

"I...you know what...you already know how I feel about your lifestyle so I'm not gonna keep beating a dead horse."

"So it ain't a problem for you to take my money to go to college but when I want to put my family in a safe home it's a crime? Is that what you telling me? 'Cause it sounds like you giving up mixed signals, Amina."

"Look, I'm not going anywhere." She paused. "This is my mother's house."

"THIS AIN'T YOUR MOTHER'S HOUSE! HOW MANY TIMES I GOTTA TELL YOU? THIS A FUCKING DOPE FIEND HANG OUT! STOP ACTING LIKE SHE BUILT THIS BITCH!"

"Daddy, what's wrong?" Naverly said walking up behind me. "Why you and mommy fighting? I'm scared."

I took a deep breath and picked her up. "I'm taking her outta this house to spend some time with daddy."

"Where you going with my baby?" Amina frowned as I walked away. "Where you going with her, Russo?"

I glared at her. "Don't ever come at me like that about what's mine too." I pointed in her face. "I said I'll be back so leave it at that." I walked out the door and slammed it shut.

TAMIKA

Tamika and Reggie were standing in their bedroom arguing about what to do about Gina. And each had their own ideas on how he should handle her. It was obvious to Tamika when she didn't come home last night that she had relapsed but Reggie wasn't willing to see it the same way.

"I know we don't have the facts yet, Reggie but shit looks awfully suspicious." She softly grabbed his hand. *"All I'm asking is that you give me the plan if she is. We can't have her in the house with my niece and—"*

"Why don't you like my mother?" He looked at her intensely. *"Because I'm not understanding at all."*

"What?"

"You heard me? What is it about my mother that rubbed you the wrong way?"

She shrugged. *"I told you already, Reggie. You talk about us being able to say anything to each other and when I do you not listening to me. She's a thief."*

"And I asked her about it and she said it was a lie." He paused. *"This shit ain't adding up to me."*

"Reggie, I saw your mother going through Russo's pockets with my own eyes. I didn't hear somebody say it. I didn't guess it. I saw her." She paused. *"Even if she didn't use the money for drugs she was gonna use it for something that she didn't want you to know about. Which is crazy because you give her everything she asks for."*

"And let me guess, you told your sister?"

THE HOUSE THAT CRACK BUILT 2

*"No." She sighed. "I was too embarrassed."
Actually she was just about to tell her yesterday
before the party but Russo and Reggie showed up
before she could. "The last thing we need is extra
drama with Drillo being gone and everything."*

*"Hey, Reggie," Gina said coming in the
doorway. "Before you say anything I'm so sorry for
being gone for so long."*

*Reggie rushed up to her and hugged her.
"Where you been, ma?" He examined her with
close eyes. "Are you okay? Were you in a car
accident or something?"*

*"Yeah, I mean no...I wasn't in an accident
but...I did let time get away from me. And I'm so
sorry about the party last night. I got up with an old
friend and celebrated me being clean. When I
looked up at the time it was five in the morning."*

*Reggie hugged her as if she had said the magic
words. In his mind things were all well.*

*But Tamika could tell in her eyes that she was
high again. "I'm just glad you okay. You had us all
worried." He looked at Tamika. "Right, bae?"*

*Tamika crossed her arms over her chest. "Yeah,
we been worried sick."*

*"You mind making me a plate of whatever was
at the party last night?" Gina asked Reggie, while*

rubbing her belly. "I'm hungry and I know you made your special steaks."

"Uh, sure, ma." He nodded. "I'll let you know when it's warm." He looked at Tamika once more and walked away.

When he left Gina strutted up to Tamika. "Sorry about whatever you did yesterday for me. With the little party and all."

"Are you really sorry?" Tamika placed her hands on her hips. "Because you have a funny way of showing it."

"Of course I am."

Tamika sneered. "You know what, Gina, you can tell him whatever you want. Just know that I don't believe shit you say out your mouth. And the moment I think he can handle it I'm gonna let him know my real feelings."

Gina smiled and shook her head a few times. "Do you love him?"

"What?" Tamika dropped her hands by her sides. "How you sound? Of course I love my husband."

"Then I'ma give you some hard advice. The last thing you wanna do is come between him and his mama. Trust me little girl, if you do that, you won't have a chance keeping him around for long."

THE HOUSE THAT CRACK BUILT 2

"How you sound? You may be his mother but I'm his wife and he will always believe me over you."

"If you believe that you have a lot to learn in this world. Now you may be a wife, and a young one at that, but don't let another, more wiser woman take him from up under you, all because you making mistakes by getting on his nerves so early. Back away from me and then back further away after that. I'm warning you." She winked and walked away.

CHAPTER FOUR

RUSSO

I wanted to treat my daughter to her favorite kid's pizza place but there were kids everywhere. It was basically an inside playground and it was driving me crazy. No matter where I turned they seemed to be bumping into me, stepping on my sneaks and getting on my nerves.

"Nigga, I ain't hearing anything you saying right now all you need to know is that I want my money by close of business."

"And what time is that?" One of my soldiers said as I watched my daughter play in a den of colorful balls. "'Cause I don't even know where I'm gonna get it from."

"That ain't my problem and you not about to visit that shit on me. You let a clown rob you and now you gotta make that back. Just don't hit my phone until you do."

I hung up on him and walked closer to the ball den. I decided to take Naverly here because I hated when she heard me arguing with her moms and it was my way of letting her know things were okay.

THE HOUSE THAT CRACK BUILT 2

It wasn't like we kept up shit all the time but still. My life was fucked up when I was her age. Both my parents left me with a dude across the street who used to rape boys and then I ended up in that house that Amina stay in. I couldn't tell her about that part of my life because it wasn't none of her business but still, it fucked me up every time I walked through those doors. Knowing that because of what I went through I'm gonna be fucked up for life.

When my phone rung I saw it was Mrs. Connelly. I figured Reggie wasn't home so she was hitting me up to do something for her at the house. I'm not gonna lie, at first I ain't like the broad but after awhile she kinda grew on me. Reminded me of the mother I never had.

"Hey, Mrs. Connelly." I shook my head because I knew she was about to ask me to do something.

"I need your help, son."

"I'm actually at the playground with Naverly." When I looked where she was playing she waved at me and I winked.

"I understand that but I need you here now." She paused. "And don't delay. Right now, son."

I frowned before looking at the phone. "What's so important where I have to drop everything?"

"Uh...I moved my refrigerator because I sprayed some roach repellant back there and now I can't put it back. Plus Reggie ain't home."

"I'll slide by your way when I'm—"

"Russo, please!" Her voice grew louder and more desperate. "Come now!"

I looked at the phone and put it back to my ear. Sometimes the old broad acted crazy and after some time I just learned it was what it was. "Aight, I'm on my way."

"Thank you."

I shook my head and dropped my phone in my pocket. "Naverly!" She was too busy jumping with the other kids so she couldn't hear me. "Aye, Naverly. Let's go."

"Five more minutes, daddy." She spread her little fingers. "Please. I made some new friends."

I winked at her. "Aight, baby girl. You got it. Five more minutes but then you have to come out here and eat your food. You haven't even touched it."

"Wow, so you really had a kid."

When I turned around I saw my ex-girlfriend Tamara looking at me. The last time I saw her she almost fucked up my situation with Amina at the diner some years back. If she was successful Amina would not be my wife and Naverly wouldn't be here either.

There was one good thing I could say for Tamara, she was definitely looking sweet. The blue jeans hugged her hips and it looked like she'd been on the beach because she glowed.

"Yeah, I got a kid." I shrugged. I could see her eyes welling up and knew she was about to cry. I had zero time for that shit. "Ah, nah, let me bounce. I already can see what type shit you on."

"I'm sorry." She grabbed my hand and I snatched away before my daughter saw her.

"It ain't nothing to be sorry for. We just over."

"Are you sure? Tell me you don't miss how I used to suck your dick just because. Or how I let you fuck me in the back of the movie theater because you got off on fucking in public. Do your girl do all that for you now?"

"My wife. Not my girl."

Her mouth hung. "You married that bitch too? What is wrong with you, Russo? She ain't supposed to be with a man like you. Why would you even choose her over me?"

I crossed my arms over my chest. "You got ten seconds. Now what you want?"

She wiped the tears rolling down her face, reached in her purse and handed me a card. "It's my num—"

"Fuck outta here with that shit." I tossed it on the ground. "Didn't you just hear me say my kid over there? If she tells my wife about this I'm—"

"Please, I just want to talk to you, Russo. I never got closure when you dumped me." She moved closer. "Please take the card and I'll leave you alone. I promise." She handed me the card again and I stuffed it in my pocket.

"Bounce."

When I looked over at Naverly she was watching me. "Daddy, can we go now?"

She seemed sad and it had me wanting to flip on my ex. "Yes, let's go." I opened the gate and helped Her put on her shoes. "But why you sad though?"

"No reason."

"Naverly...Never lie to daddy."

"I peed on myself."

I looked down at her jeans and saw they were wet. I lifted her up and raised her chin. "Hey, don't you dare hold your head down. It's okay.

You just gotta be careful next time. Don't play so much that you wet on yourself."

Tears rolled down her face and from the corner of my eye my worst nightmare was being realized. Two masked men were aimed and firing in my direction.

I tossed my daughter back in the ball den, released the gun from my waist and fired with all my life.

CHAPTER FIVE

TAMIKA

*T*amika was prepping the baked chicken for tonight's dinner when Gina walked inside. She immediately strutted toward the mashed potatoes, grabbed the spoon and started to stir.

"Can you please not touch that," Tamika asked with a harsh attitude. "You didn't even wash your hands."

"Girl, I been cooking longer than you been alive." Gina snapped. "The last thing you want to do is try to tell me how to cook. Stay in your lane."

"So that mean we gotta eat dirt?" Tamika rolled her eyes. "Like I said, Gina, I have it." Tamika snatched the ladle out of her hand and looked at her sternly. She immediately noticed cocaine on her nose. "And instead of messing with dinner you may wanna get that off your face." She pointed at it.

Gina's eyes widened and she quickly wiped her nostrils. "It was powder."

"I know."

"I'm talking about baby powder."

Tamika shook her head. "Ain't no need in you lying to me. Reggie don't believe nothing I say anyway." She shrugged and opened the oven door to check the chicken before closing it again.

"Maybe you should stop feeding his head with lies."

"You a bad influence on my family and I want that to stop. So if you call that lies I have no intention on not speaking my mind."

"Maybe you should look at me different instead of turning your back on your husband's mother." She tilted her head to the left. "And trying to tear us apart."

"Just leave me alone and stay outta of my way, Gina."

Gina paused and looked crazily. "You are so fucking judgmental. You have no idea about what I've gone through."

Tamika looked at her and tried to search her heart for compassion. "Then tell me. The last thing I wanna be is fighting with you." Tamika moved closer. "Maybe you are a better person than I'm giving you credit for. And if that's true it's my fault for not trying to be close. But you have to talk to me, Gina. And you have to be honest about what you're doing."

Gina stood in the middle of the kitchen, her face reddening as she battled with telling her how much of a good mother she was until a few bad choices and even more bad men changed her for the worst.

"I love Reggie." She said as tears rolled down her face. Her eyes staring at nothing in particular. "And I don't deserve his unconditional love and I want nothing more than to change but I need some help. I need to get away from...Frank."

"Maybe I can help you." Tamika placed her hand on her own belly, trying to stop her stomach from flipping.

"But how?"

"Prayer. Fighting for you. Going with you to rehab." Tamika began crying too. "You're family now so something has to work, it just has too." She wiped tears away. "And whatever we choose will work if we do it together."

"You think so?"

Tamika was so happy she was opening up that she gripped her mother-in-law into a loving hug. "I know so." She released her. "I had a really good mother who taught me a lot about life. I may not have always listened but I heard enough."

Gina looked at her closer and then snatched away. "So what you saying...That your mother was better than me?"

"What? No...of course not. I—"

"Then what are you saying?"

"Look, I made a mistake saying anything about my mother." She took a deep breath to gather her thoughts to try to appeal to her again. "I was just trying to say—"

"Do you know what a roach tastes like?" She paused. "Ever feel it squishing in your food?"

Tamika frowned. "What...no, of course not!"

"Well I have. And it's bitter, and Reggie and I ate more of them then you could imagine when we didn't have enough money for new food and so roaches took over everything else. But we were too hungry to fight to pick them out so we let them stay."

"Gina—"

"No, you listen to me! I ain't lead no privileged life. I made some mistakes but when it came to that boy I did all I could."

"And you can do more." Tamika's chest rose and fell rapidly. "Right now by getting clean. Please."

"You think it's so easy," Gina continued. "You better hope you never have to experience anything like this."

"I won't."

"Never say never."

"What's going on?" Reggie asked bopping into the kitchen after seeing them so close together.

Gina walked up to her. "I don't want to say anything but your wife has left me no choice."

Tamika frowned, totally confused by what she was about to say.

"What you mean, ma?" He asked.

"Your wife...she...um...hit me, Reggie." She breathed heavily. "Slapped me because I was trying to help cook."

Tamika stumbled backward. "That's a lie."

"See, this is why I didn't want to say anything," Gina continued. "Maybe I should just leave and never come back."

"No!" He yelled grabbing her arm. "Don't go...let me...let me just talk to my wife."

"But she's gonna lie on me, Reggie! I mean don't you see what she's trying to do? She's trying to tear you away from me. She doesn't want us to have a relationship."

THE HOUSE THAT CRACK BUILT 2

"Just go to my room and let me talk to her." He hugged her and then held up her chin. *"Just don't leave. We only just found each other and I don't want to lose you again."*

She grinned. *"Okay, honey."* And walked away.

He walked deeper into the kitchen. *"She's lying, Reggie."*

"But why would she do that? What would be the purpose?"

"I don't know!" She threw her hands up. *"But she obviously doesn't want us to be together."*

"My mother loves our relationship."

"The woman is an addict!" She pointed at the direction she walked in. *"And a liar at best!"*

"Tamika, don't—"

"No! Don't tell me anything other than you believe me. Ever since you came into my life I made a decision to be better for you, prettier for you. And stronger for you, we have never lied to one another. I would never hurt you because you don't deserve anything but the best from me. And I'm telling you that your mother is lying. So who do you believe? Me or her?"

"Tamika."

"Now, Reggie! I need to know now."

He took a deep breath and looked around before settling on her eyes again. "I have to see how she's doing." He kissed her on the lips. "I'm sorry. I just..." He walked away.

Tamika slid down on the floor and cried.

GINA

After overhearing them, Gina rushed out the house and toward the block. But Reggie was on her Trail eager to talk to her before she got too far away. "Ma, don't leave like this. And where you going anyway? I thought we were about to eat dinner together."

"I'm going somewhere where I don't have to be around your wife!" She paused. "Because I can't take it right now, Reggie. She's gonna be the cause of me getting back on drugs."

"Ma, don't say that."

"Leave me alone, Reggie! And don't try and follow me either."

THE HOUSE THAT CRACK BUILT 2

She ran away and an hour later Gina was with Frank getting high in an alleyway. "I told you I'm the only one who loves you." *Frank said with wide crazy eyes.* "Maybe one day you'll realize that and stop looking for something in your son that isn't there anymore."

"I know, Frank!" *Her knees felt weak and she hunched a little.* "You don't have to keep telling me every time I see you."

"I know I'm hurting your feelings but don't go back to him, Gina." *She paused.* "Stay with me, where you belong."

"You're forgetting he's the only one who can give us money." *She paused.* "Because in case you don't realize, we basically broke."

"We can make money." *He shrugged as if it were the easiest thing in the world.* "We always do."

"Don't you mean I can make money? Because whenever we're short I'm the one who has to sleep with people to get it back."

"So now you blaming me for being in this predicament?"

"I didn't say that."

"You know what, maybe I should just leave." He got up to walk away but she stopped him by grabbing his hand.

"I'm not saying that, Frank! I'll get the money if I have too. Just please don't leave me anymore. Every time we fight you make a move to leave and that makes me feel like I can't trust you."

"Call me crazy, but I'm starting to think I would be better off without you." He walked away again and this time she let him go.

CHAPTER SIX

AMINA

When I walked downstairs I saw Tamika playing with Naverly on the sofa. I was glad because I needed her to watch her while I went out looking for Russo. Earlier today he dropped her off and then went back out without telling me where he was going. Something he never did. At first I thought he was still mad at me for not wanting to leave this house but now I think it was something else.

"Mind doing me a big favor?" I asked, smiling widely. "Something that would mean a whole, whole, whole bunch to me?"

She smirked. "Girl, go 'head and leave. Just bring me back some butter pecan ice cream."

I smiled widely. "Are you sure?"

"Yes I'm sure." She tickled Naverly again who broke out into laughter. "We were gonna order a pizza and watch movies anyway. Go do what you gotta do."

"But it's a Saturday. Don't you and Reggie usually have date night? I thought you would be—"

"I said I'll watch her, Amina." She snapped. "Just leave it at that. Okay?"

I threw my hands up in the air. "Whoa...I was just joking anyway. But I do appreciate you watching her."

She took a deep breath. "Look, I'm sorry to snap. But a lot of stuff been going on and...I guess I kinda don't wanna talk about it. Not right now anyway."

I nodded and looked around. "Where is Reg?"

"With his mother I guess. I think they went out to eat to spend some mother and son time together. Like that's even a real thing."

I giggled. "But we got leftovers in the fridge from her party."

"I know, Amina. Please just go."

I walked toward the door and grabbed my purse. Before leaving out for some reason I felt like I needed to say more. So I said, "I love you. Very much."

She smiled. "I know."

"I love you too, mommy!" Naverly blurted out, sending us both into heavy laughter.

When I pulled up to the mansion Russo's car was parked in the driveway. I entered the code to the gate, drove in and parked behind his BMW. I was surprised that he was even here because even though he always said if he wasn't at my house, he would be here instead of running the streets, sometimes Russo lies. Most times about small things but sometimes about bigger things too.

Using my key I walked inside and saw him lying on the sofa in the living room, drinking Hennessey out a glass. "What's going on?"

"Nothing." He sounded dry, like he could care less if I was in the house or not.

I put my purse on the table and sat next to him. "This right here...whatever it is...ain't right."

"Meaning?"

"You married, Russo. You can't just leave and go places without telling me." I paused. "And you can't not talk to me either. I mean, did something happen today when you were with Naverly?"

He stared at me. "If I say something to you. Something very important. Do you think you could possibly have an open mind? No matter what you hear?"

"Yes."

"Are you sure?"

I laughed. "Russo, you act like I haven't accepted it all, already. Short of my baby being put in a fucked up situation, which is why I don't want us to live here, I dealt with it all right?"

He nodded, sat his glass down and moved closer. "I'm glad you came over."

I giggled. "Like I was really gonna let my husband stay over here without me."

"You know I was coming back right?"

"No...that's why I'm here. We fought and then you took Naverly out, brought her back and stayed out."

He nodded and leaned in and kissed me. The bitter taste of the liquor on his tongue for some reason got me excited. "I want some of that pussy now."

He moved closer, undid my jeans and pushed them to the floor. Next he removed my panties and my cheeks pressed against the sofa as he pried my legs open and lowered his head to lick me softly. Don't get me wrong, Russo loved eating pussy but lately he would only do it if I didn't reach an orgasm after he came.

I touched the sides of his face, widened my legs and pumped softly into his lips. "Russo...mmmmm...this feels so good."

"You taste good too," he mumbled.

"Please don't stop." I pumped a little more onto his face.

He pushed my leg a little wider open before stretching his tongue from the entry of my asshole to the tip of my clit. "Damn, you taste so sweet."

I was trying not to cum but he was doing it not only like he wanted it but like his life depended on it. Every limb of my body trembled as I tried to make it last forever. "Russo, come up here so we can cum together."

"Nah, this for you. I'm good."

I looked down at him. "You...you...sure?"

"Yeah, baby. I just wanna taste that cum." He flipped my clit a few more times with his tongue and before I knew it I came all in his mouth. When I was done he kissed me softly on the neck and then my lips.

"Wow, that was...it felt so good," I said trying to catch my breath. "You just...you just...took everything away."

"I need to do that more often." He said slyly. "Because you deserve that shit."

I smiled and then looked at him seriously. "What you do? You might as well come clean."

He giggled. "Nothing."

I looked at him with a lowered gaze. "You sure?"

"You got the keys to my house and my ring, Amina. When I say I'm not doing nothing that's exactly what I mean. If you don't believe me feel free to check."

"Everything about what you just said is wrong." I paused. "Your house is with me. And this is just a...a dream. All it's gonna take is the FEDS getting involved and they can take all this. But they can never take away your family."

"If this is a dream it's a good one." He said jokingly.

"I was thinking more like a nightmare."

RING. RING. RING.

I slipped my panties back on and grabbed my cell phone from my purse. It was from a number I didn't recognize and I frowned.

THE HOUSE THAT CRACK BUILT 2

"Everything okay?" He asked.

"Yeah...just don't know who calling." I continued to look at the number, for what I don't know. Maybe I sensed that whoever was calling was about to ruin my night.

"Well answer it," Russo said.

I answered the phone. "Hell...hello."

"Hey, sis."

Oh no. It was Drillo. I frowned and looked at Russo. "Who this?" I don't know why I asked because I'd know my brother's voice anywhere. Maybe I was hoping he'd lie and maybe even go away.

"It's me. Drillo. And I need a big favor."

CHAPTER SEVEN

RUSSO

I had a lot on my mind and the last thing I felt like doing was dealing with this lil' nigga. I'm out here with real shit on my head and...then he calls my wife talking about he got locked up again. He was driving me crazy.

Fuck!

"I could've scooped him myself," I said to Reggie who was sitting in the passenger seat. We decided to get him and leave the wives at home since neither of them wanted to see him anyway. I guess they were tired of all the empty promises. He was an adult now and he was on his own.

"Nah, I need the break." He looked ahead and then focused back on his phone.

I nodded and looked over at him. "You sound like me. You got trouble in paradise?"

He shook his head and ran his hand down his face. It was all the answer I needed. "Nothing like it."

"Wanna rap about it?"

"To tell you the truth, the way I feel right now, I don't even think it'll matter."

THE HOUSE THAT CRACK BUILT 2

"I feel you." I paused. "Oh, that dude I wanted you to meet canceled so don't worry about it tonight. I still got your payday though since you got the pack."

"Thanks, man." He sighed. "'Cause I gotta get my mother out the house because shit ain't connecting the way I wanted it to."

"Oh, Tamika ain't been feeling her?"

"Understatement of the year." He paused. "I don't know what's going on to tell you the truth." He paused again. "I walked in the other day on 'Mika cooking and the next thing I know moms saying she slapped her for no reason."

I laughed.

"What's funny?" He asked.

"You don't believe that shit do you? That your wife slapped your mother? I mean really...sounds far fetched don't you think?"

"What...I mean...how you figure?"

"Listen, I don't know your mother. And I would never call her a liar. But one thing I do know is that your wife would never lay hands on her for no reason. Or try to fuck up anything. She loves you too much to do something so foul."

"I know but...she said she did hit her. What I'm supposed to do? Not believe moms?"

"I'ma leave that one alone." I said not really feeling like going deeper. "And this nigga hitting us up at the wrong time. As if we don't have enough shit on our plate."

"I know. Did he say why they locked him up this time? Seems like it's always something."

"Nah." I paused. "And Amina ain't ask either."

"What you wanna do about him?"

"I'm thinking about it as we speak." I gritted my teeth. "But my spirit says to press that temple."

He rotated his head quickly in my direction. "Don't go that far. He still blood."

"Whose blood?" I laughed once. "Mine?"

"Your wife's."

"Exactly. And that's why putting that nigga out his misery would be a sweet deal. Look at how much paper we left hanging around the crib for him to steal. He breaking in doors, crashing in windows. That's the part that gets me. They don't want to see their own brother so bad that they prefer he steals from us."

Reggie shrugged. "All I'm saying is..."

"Look, you my man, and I fuck with you, but save your breath. Whatever decisions I make when I see that nigga is my own."

THE HOUSE THAT CRACK BUILT 2

Reggie raised his hands in the air. "Say no more."

We were parked in front of the jail when Drillo crawled in the backseat. He smelled of urine, shit and problems. I adjusted my rearview mirror and looked at him.

"Thanks again, man," he said. "For bailing me out and stuff." He looked at Reggie and tapped his shoulder. "Oh, I ain't see you right there. How you been man?"

Reggie nodded and continued to text on his cell. "I'm good."

"So where my sisters?" He asked. "Are they meeting up with us later?"

"Nah. They ain't coming." I pulled off.

"So where we going then? To the house?"

"Nah. Like I said, they ain't coming and we ain't meeting them either."

He nodded. "Look, I can tell you mad at me but like I was telling the dudes in there, I'm done with using, man. This was the last straw.

Like...like having to live on the streets and not have a place to go...it just makes me see the world differently."

"Is that right?"

"Yeah. I'm going straight." He paused. "But I'ma need your help. Everybody's really. Because the devil be calling me you know?"

"But I thought you were gay." I said. "How you going straight?

Reggie looked at me. "Come on, man."

"It's okay," Drillo said. "I can take a joke. I have too. I mean look at my life."

I laughed. "You need to take a look at your life. Because everything about you is comedy."

He sat back and crossed his arms over his chest. "I just wanna see my sisters. Nothing else matters."

"Oh, is that where you think we're going? To the crib?"

"Aren't we?"

"Not even close."

He sat up. "So where you taking me again?"

I leaned back more and continued to handle my ride.

"Russo, where you taking me, man?"

THE HOUSE THAT CRACK BUILT 2

We were standing in some woods off of the beltway going toward Delaware. Drillo was on his knees and Reggie was pacing some feet away as I held the gun to his head. Drillo on the other hand was crying his eyes out.

"Give me one reason why I shouldn't kill you." I pressed it to his dome. "Just one that would convince me that your life is worth something. Because right now I think the world would be better off without you."

"Please, man, I'm begging you." He raised his hands in the air. "I'ma get clean."

"I don't believe you, nigga!" I said through clenched teeth. "You been saying that shit for ages. What's different now?"

"Because I really want to be clean. I'm begging you, man." Snot oozed out his nose and rested on his lip. "All I wanna do is be better for my family. So I can see my niece and—"

"Not a good enough reason." I cocked the weapon and squeezed the trigger.

"NOOOOO!" Reggie screamed.

When he walked over to me Drillo had pissed himself again but he was still alive. I reached in my pocket, pulled out all the cash I had on me and threw it at him, it dampened with his urine. "Never call or come by my wife again unless you clean. And best believe I got a million ways of finding out, most which will hurt."

I tapped Reggie on the shoulder and we both walked to the car, him looking back once. "Did you have to do that shit, man? You went way overboard...way overboard. What if the girls find out?"

"Look, I'm dealing with a lot, Reg." I paused. "And I can't have him on the sidelines making my load heavier. So the answer to your question is yes. I had to do that and I could've done more. And I'm capable of more. Be glad I didn't. So let's leave it alone."

We pulled off, leaving him stranded.

CHAPTER EIGHT

RUSSO

I pulled up in front of Mrs. Connelly's house exhausted. Amina had me running around the grocery store all day for stuff I'm pretty sure she had in the house already. Normally I'd leave Reggie to those things but he was still mad at me for how I did Drillo the other day. I told him he may not feel me today but he'll understand in the future. At the end of the day the last person you want in your life is a dope head who is unwilling to change. A person like that is like a bad apple, contaminating everybody.

I was just about to go into her house when I got a call. It was one of my soldiers. I pulled my cell phone from my pocket and placed it against my ear. For some reason I felt like this would be bad news but I couldn't be sure. "What up, man. I'm kinda busy right now. Whatever you got to say make it quick."

"It will be. Look, man, you gotta be careful."

I sat up. "That's already a characteristic about me. But why you telling me now though?"

"Because I think you being hunted." He paused. "And I got it on good authority too."

"From one of my people?"

"Nah. And that's all I can say."

I laughed once. "Well did they tell you by who?"

"I don't know all that either, man. It's all the info I could find."

I took a deep breath. I already knew somebody had a price on my head after what happened at the Big Mouse Pizza but I hoped I was in the wrong place at the wrong time. Now I know that hit was definitely in my name.

"Aight, man. Thanks for the info."

"Oh...before I forget. The boy Reg is straight up. Good pick."

"Already know. But why you say that?"

"He stole some nigga in the jaw earlier today for shorting him on your paper. When the nigga hit the pavement he crawled on top of him and finished him off. Yo was out cold."

I nodded. "Oh yeah. He told me about that." I lied. I figured he was letting off some steam after what happened with Drillo.

"Aight, well I'm out."

THE HOUSE THAT CRACK BUILT 2

I tossed the cell in the passenger seat, took a deep breath and ran my hand down my face. I need some answers on why my life been going fucked up lately but I knew there was nothing I could do about it. Out here you all for self. Ain't no God looking out for niggas like my wife believe. It's just us and this world and I was sure of it.

I knocked on the door and Mrs. Connelly smiled and pulled me inside. Her house smelled of baked cookies and cakes. She was getting older. I saw more wrinkles than I had when I first moved around here but her eyes were always the same. Like she could see your lies before you got a chance to say 'em.

"Sorry I couldn't get here until now. I been real busy and I'm not gonna even kick you a bunch of details because you know my situation."

"You're right. And it's okay."

"Did you get help with whatever you needed?"

"Yes and no." She sat down and poured tea into a pink and white cup that matched the pot. "But have a seat, Russo. I still wanna talk to you about a few things."

"Yes and no?" I repeated. "What that mean?"

"Reggie saw about the things I needed done in my house but I been waiting to lay eyes on you too. Now have a seat. You're treating me like we're strangers when we're anything but."

I cleared my throat. "I'm here now." I sat down.

"Why didn't you come when I called the other day? You used to be so careful when it came to me."

I thought about getting shot at and the fact that although I liked Mrs. Connelly, I already had a wife. "Too much to tell. It's a blessing I'm here today though."

"I know."

My eyebrows rose. "You know about what?"

"Well I can't say that I know what exactly happened pursay, but I do know that something bad was in the wind for you. Had you come when I called you could've avoided it."

I laughed but not hard because for real the old bird was spooking me out. "So you saying you knew something was gonna happen before it did?"

"Was I wrong?" She smiled, like she saw the entire day even though she wasn't there.

I cleared my throat. "You know what, I don't even believe in all that. No offense."

She laughed and sipped her tea. "If you don't believe in something more intelligent than yourself you a fool. I'm telling you I got a bad vibe and it was so strong it had me wanting to call you right away."

It was time for me to bounce so I got up. "Well, I'm about to leave. You got trash or—"

"You got people praying for you, son. And whenever you got people sending out energy to your well being, whether you know it or not, every method necessary for your safety will be used. Even if it means bothering old women like me in my dreams."

"Mrs. Connelly, I—"

"Slow down, boy. Slow all the way down. Your life is coming up short. And—"

"Mrs. C, with all due respect, this shit you talking about ain't got nothing to do with—"

I don't even know how she reached me that fast. But before I knew it she slapped me so hard I buckled back. I almost released my hammer on her before I came to my senses but I had to put her in line. "Never put your hands on me again."

"And never disrespect me like that again."

I took a deep breath. "You know what..." I just walked out. The moment I reached my car I saw my wife bolting toward me.

Now what?

"We need to talk right now!" She was out of breath and looked like she'd been crying. Maybe she heard about what I did to her kid brother. If that was true I had plans to find that little nigga and...well...let's just say it wouldn't be pretty.

"What you wanna talk about now, Amina? Because this is shaping up to be a pretty fucked up day."

She looked over my shoulder. "You wanna do this in private or in front of the entire block?"

I looked behind me, back at my wife and said, "FUCK IT! LET'S GO!"

THE HOUSE THAT CRACK BUILT 2

CHAPTER NINE

REGGIE

*A*s Reggie lie on top of Tamika, his dick tucked softly in her body he looked down into her eyes. *The love they had was the stuff of dreams and yet because they were young, they were at the mercy of any passing suspicion or problems. They would need to stand strong together if they were going to last.*

And right now things didn't look good.

"I love you," he said. "So fucking much, bae. I wanna us to stop fighting and shit. This ain't for us."

She smiled. "Me too, Reggie." *She moaned.* "You feel so good like this. Just me and you. Alone."

"I don't know what I would do without you." *He continued.* "Not trying to find out either."

"Let's not think about stuff like that." *She kissed him, sliding her wet tongue between his lips.* "Whenever you say those words it makes me...sick to the stomach. I just want us to be forever. Last forever. Love forever. I love being your wife."

"And you gonna stay my wife."

She smiled brighter and then it drifted away slowly. Her expression grew serious as if something was weighing on her heart and mind and at the moment it was.

"What is it, Mika?" He paused. "I'm too heavy?" He was about to get up but she grabbed him.

"No...stay right there. Please."

"Then what's on your mind?"

She shrugged and moved her hips a little. "Let's play again."

"Don't say that," he kissed her neck. "'Cause I can def' go another round."

"Then let's do it." She said seductively. "As a matter of fact lets fuck all night. Only taking a break to eat."

"We will, after you answer my question." He kissed her lips again. "You always say I don't listen and now I'm here. Tell me what it is."

"There's nothing wrong, Reggie. As a matter of fact all I wanna do is be the positive in your life. I don't want you having to worry about what I'm gonna say or do before you come home."

"Happy couples argue too."

"But why?" She said passionately. "Who says that? If two people have a disagreement and they

THE HOUSE THAT CRACK BUILT 2

love each other, like me and you, why can't we disagree but talk it out, while still respecting each other?"

He grinned. "Damn, you really growing up."

"I be reading and stuff I guess." She shrugged. "All I know is without you, I'll drown."

"What the..."

"I'm serious. After I was raped you came right into my life. And sometimes I think I don't think about that night because I feel safe with you. If you were to leave me how I know things won't get dark again?"

"I'm not leaving. Ever."

"Do you promise?" A tear rolled backwards and into the mattress. "Because I need to know you'll be here no matter what."

He raised her chin. "Look at me." She turned her head softly and he put it back. "No, I want you to look at me, Tamika. Because I need you to see I'm being nothing but real right now."

She turned her head softly.

"I am never leaving you, ever," he paused. "We may fight and I wish I could say that we won't but I know that's not true. I never knew anybody who didn't have a disagreement or two. But what I do know is this, just like you say I saved you, you saved me too. I'm not letting that go for—"

"Damn, son," Gina said opening the door without knocking. "You ain't make her weak in the knees yet?"

Reggie rose up and they both covered their bodies with the sheets. Neither could believe she was that ridiculous as to come into their room. "Ma, what you doing in here?"

"Just asking a—"

"Get out!" Tamika yelled. "Now!"

She rolled her eyes and slammed the door.

Tamika popped up in bed, her breasts exposed. "I want her out, Reggie."

"Come on, bae. She was just—"

"You just made love to me not even a second ago. And in that time you said you would never leave me. Well if you don't put her out of our home then you gonna have to, Reggie. Because I can't live with her another day. I just can't!"

"Tamika, you—"

"I want her out!" She jumped up, snatched her red robe off the chair and stormed out.

"Is everything okay?" Amina asked standing in the doorway. "Because I could hear ya'll fighting downstairs."

Reggie covered his exposed dick. "Yeah...but can you close that door? I'ma...I'ma handle everything. I promise."

Amina complied and Reggie screamed into his palm.

"Ma, why would you come in my room without knocking?" Reggie asked in the backyard of the house.

"What? I didn't know you were—"

"Don't say you didn't know we were having sex because you said it when you came inside. You said, ma." He tucked his hands into his grey sweatpants. His bare chest out. "Now you got her madder than ever. I'm not understanding why you would even do that."

"You already know she don't like me, Reggie. So don't act like I made anything worse than it already is."

"Nah, we not doing that this time, ma." He pointed at the ground. "This is different and you were way out of line."

"So now you really taking her side so I guess you want me just gone huh?"

"My wife has a right to have a certain amount of privacy in her home and you took that away, ma. Now you know I stand by you but not when you wrong."

Gina began to cry heavily. "I knew you wouldn't love me if I came back. Everybody said I should stay away because I did too much damage and...and I said no because I want to build a relationship with my son. And now that I'm back everything is conspiring to tear us apart."

"Don't say that." He pulled her to him. "You know I want you in my life."

"But your wife doesn't." She snatched away from him. "You gotta make a decision, Reggie. Me or her."

His eyebrows rose. "Wait...are you serious?"

"You gotta make a decision and you gotta do it now. Because I'm not gonna be in your life if I feel like you don't want me there. I'm sorry that I have to do this but this is the case. My sobriety depends on it."

Reggie walked away, his bare toes pressing into the damp grass. He looked at the house across from where he was, the one he grew up in. So

THE HOUSE THAT CRACK BUILT 2

many memories both bad and good flooded his mind. Prior to meeting Tamika he just knew he would be stuck over there forever. In fact, the plan was to find his mother and if she was still on drugs, he was going to kill himself.

But God answered his prayers when Tamika came into his world. Two lost souls trying to find their way to God.

"Reggie, what's it gonna be?"

"You, mama. I choose you."

CHAPTER TEN

AMINA

We were in my house and I was trying to understand why once again Russo had failed to tell me the truth. It was like I couldn't trust him anymore and it made me uncomfortable. "Russo, why didn't you tell me?" I asked pacing in the living room as he leaned against the wall.

"There was nothing to say." He pulled out his phone and began texting. "It happened and we safe so just leave it at that. Plus I'm getting tired of feeling like I have to always explain myself to you."

I walked closer. I couldn't believe my husband was acting like being with our daughter during a shoot out was not a problem. Or worse, that he didn't have to tell me. "So you just gonna act like it was okay? And nothing happened?"

"You know that's not what I'm saying. That shit had me bent ever since but still!"

"Then what should I think. You not even—"

"Why the fuck you keep coming at me like this shit ain't fuck me up?" He moved off the wall and

THE HOUSE THAT CRACK BUILT 2

got in my face. "Huh? Don't you know the guilt I been putting myself through ever since that shit happened."

"Russo, I—"

"Nah, you wanted to hear what I have to say so I'm gonna give it to you. I got in a situation that got out of control. But understand this, they won't catch me slipping again."

I looked at him, rolled my eyes and flopped on the sofa. Throwing my face in my hands I breathed deeply. "Russo, you can't take her outta this house no more. Not until whatever you got going on goes away."

He walked over to me, one of his fist clenched tightly. "Are you asking me or telling me?"

"Does it matter?"

"You my wife and you gotta ask me something like that?" He tilted his head slightly. "Am I hearing you right?"

"She was in danger, Russo. Our baby girl was in danger and she could've been shot over some shit that wasn't even her fault. And now you acting like you mad at me."

"I ain't mad at you. I—"

"You know what, Russo, just get up out my face." I got up, grabbed my purse off the ledge and was about to walk out the door. "Because I'm not about to go back and forth with you on this."

"Who you think you disrespecting?"

I turned around. "What?"

"I'm talking to you, and you just gonna walk out the door?" He moved closer and for some reason I thought he was about to hit me. "Is that the type of nigga you thought you had? One you could talk to like you ain't got sense?"

My heart was pounding. Russo never hit me or even acted like he wanted to but now I couldn't be sure. "Russo, I need to go."

"And I get all that but we were having a conversation."

"I'm listening, Russo."

He walked closer. "You right, I shouldn't have hid that from you. I should've come to you the moment it happened but I didn't want you worrying about it because it's street shit and like I said I got it under control. And at the end of the day you gonna have to trust me. That's the bottom line."

I nodded.

"But I'm sorry, Mina." He continued. "I'll never hide something like that from you again."

I looked into his eyes, angry with everything. "Can I go now?"

He let my hand go and I stormed out.

I pulled my BMW up in front of my old apartment complex. I don't know what made me drive down here, I guess I just wanted to be near my mother's presence, even if the last time we were here my sister was raped.

All of a month ago I thought I had an ideal life. I was married to a man who loved me and told me how pretty I was every night and my daughter was healthy, happy and loved. But now I was realizing it wasn't as perfect as I thought. Russo was a drug dealer and at first I thought I could deal with it but now I'm not so sure.

I was about to pull off when I looked up the street and saw my cousin April standing on the corner. Confused, I pulled up to her and rolled down my window. She looked bad. Her hair was matted, her face was soiled and her clothes looked dingy.

"April, is that you?"

She leaned down. "Amina?" She said excitedly before pulling the door and getting inside.

The moment she sat in my car it smelled so bad I thought I would throw up. It made things worse when she reached over and hugged my neck, causing me to inhale her body odor even more.

"What's going on with you?"

She shrugged. "A lot, Amina! Daddy got locked up for trying to sell prescription drugs to get crack and...we got kicked out. So I'm homeless."

"But what about...your boyfriend...I mean...my ex?"

"He dumped me a long time ago. For real it was right after we saw you in the mall." She sighed and her breath smelled so bad it made my stomach churn. "Kept saying he should've never got with me." She shook her head. "But I'm so used to being the consolation prize so it don't even matter anymore."

"So you living out on the streets?" I couldn't believe how soiled and dirty she looked. I never saw my cousin like this before. Despite it all, she was still pretty.

"Where else I'm gonna go?"

THE HOUSE THAT CRACK BUILT 2

I sighed. "I'll take you to my house to get cleaned up and then I'll rent you a room."

Her eyebrows rose. "For real?"

"Yeah." I shrugged. "Why not?"

"Because of all that stuff I did to you."

I sighed. "Yeah, everything in me saying not to bring you in my house. But when my mother died I started to understand the importance of family. I mean, you falling on hard times now and at the end of the day you need me."

"But ain't you messing with Russo?" She paused. "Because that's what the streets been saying."

"Yeah...we still together. But what does that have to do with me helping you out?"

"Nothing really. I just heard about what he do to niggas he don't know. He may not want me to be staying by you."

"Look, let me work on and worry about my husband." I paused. "Shit will pan out."

"Wait...he your husband?" She asked with wider eyes. "You married that RICH NIGGA!"

"Yeah, I guess." I put my car in drive. "But that's a whole extra story."

She put her seatbelt on. "Well fill my ears up! I ain't got nothing but time."

CHAPTER ELEVEN

AMINA

My fingers were tight from cleaning Gina's apartment all day. Reggie rented her a new place in downtown Baltimore, and furnished every room. Although it was supposed to be a happy time something felt off. For starters I was barely talking to Russo and he was barely talking to me. And then Reggie was barely talking to Tamika and although Tamika tried to reach out to him, she said nothing to his mother.

Tension was rising in our house and for some reason I knew it was bound to get worse.

"Thank you for helping," Gina said walking into the kitchen where I was putting up her new plates. "Reggie bought me more stuff than I need. I think he forgot I'm living alone."

"What about that guy who came by but left when he saw we needed help setting up?"

She smiled. "He's just a friend."

I closed the cabinet and turned around to face her. "Well, we don't mind helping. That's what family is for right?"

"Well if I can help you with anything in the future too let me know." She paused. "I may not have a lot to offer financially but I'll make up for it in other ways."

"Okay, well you can start by telling me what's going on with you and my sister."

She laughed.

I didn't.

"Wait, you serious?" She continued. "I...I don't know what you mean." She was lying and it was all over her face.

"Nobody tells me anything anymore and I'm starting to get sick of it." I paused. "So I was hoping you could clear some things up."

She took a deep breath. "Let's just say your sister is spreading lies about me and my life."

I frowned. "To who?"

"My son."

"Well what is she saying exactly? Because I know my sister. And even if she is saying things she means well."

"Well it's crazy really." She took a deep breath again. "I feel bad even repeating it but she is telling people that I'm using drugs.

I laughed. "And you are."

She coughed. "What...what are you talking about?"

"Gina, I saw you doing drugs this morning in your bedroom. Right before the movers brought in your bedroom set. And I saw you doing drugs at the house, right when you made a decision to leave. You were in my backyard."

"Well, if you really believe that why didn't you say anything? To me or Reggie?"

"Because things were already in motion for you to bounce." I shrugged. "What would I look like saying anything when shit was already moving for the best?"

She shook her head. "I can't even believe all this."

"What's there to believe?" I paused. "You want to be an addict and now you got the space to do it. But trust me, you got about a year in you before you lose everything you have."

"Everything cool?" Tamika asked walking into the kitchen.

Gina rolled her eyes at both of us and walked out, pushing past my sister on the way.

"Let me guess," Tamika said, "She hates you too now."

THE HOUSE THAT CRACK BUILT 2

"Yep." I paused. "But what do I care? She's out of our house and peace has been returned. Right?"

We both laughed. "So when you wanted to tell me something the other day, it was about her using drugs?"

"Wait, you found out?"

"Tamika, I found out in a crazy way. But why didn't you just tell me? You know Naverly in the house and impressionable and stuff."

"You right and I don't know." She took a deep breath and hopped on the counter. "I was embarrassed I guess."

"But she could've...exposed my daughter to that shit. And you have to understand, I can't have her be impressed with any foolishness. Definitely not with an addict in our house."

"I know. That's why I put my foot down with Reggie. Except now he isn't talking to me anymore." She sighed. "But let's talk about why you let April in the house. After she fucked your last man."

"Because she needs help."

"But we wouldn't even help Drillo."

"Correction." I pointed at her. "We tried to help Drillo but he kept going back on drugs. Plus I don't even know if that's what she's doing. I really just think she's homeless."

She shook her head. "What is wrong with us? Why is trouble following everywhere we go nowadays?"

"Everything's done." Reggie said entering the door. "She says she has friends to help her later."

Tamika hopped off the counter and walked toward him. "Can we talk? In private?"

"I'm not in the mood." He kissed her cheek. "Maybe later. Okay?"

Tamika nodded and he walked away. Slowly I moved toward her. "Anything else I can do?"

"Nah. Just...give me a hug."

I hugged her tightly and she cried in my arms.

We were sitting in Russo's pickup truck waiting on Reggie to come downstairs. It had been about fifteen minutes and at first I don't think nobody noticed because we were all on our phones. I was texting April to ask how things were going at the house since she was babysitting. She said they were good and wondered if Naverly could have the cookies she'd been asking for.

Tamika was talking to one of her friends from college and Russo seemed to be deep in his phone too. But I wasn't about to sit in this car forever either. "Mika, maybe you should hit Reggie to find out where he is."

"I did. He's not answering though." She paused and looked at the building. "Earlier his phone was dead so."

"I'll go get him." Russo said.

"No...I'll go." Tamika opened the door and walked out.

TAMIKA

Tamika knocked on the door and Gina opened it up. "We waiting for Reggie to come down." She looked over her shoulder. "Can you tell him to come out so we can go home?"

"Oh...I forgot to tell you. He's staying the night."

Her eyes widened. "What? Why?"

Reggie walked up to the door. "I got it, ma." She smiled at him and walked away. "I'm staying over, bae."

"Reggie, that's something you should've said to me in private. So we could talk about it like a couple." She paused. "You don't just do stuff like this."

"I did tell you. I mean are you sure?" He scratched his head. "Because I swore I brought it up to you when we were moving stuff inside."

"No, you didn't, Reggie. You didn't. What if I had a problem with this? What if I wanted you home?"

"I'm sorry, babes because I thought I did say something. I just want to get her settled in and—"

"You know what, fuck you!" Tamika ran away crying.

CHAPTER TWELVE

AMINA

When we got back to the house Russo had to nudge me awake. And when I looked back at Tamika she looked like she was still crying. Her eyes were red and her face was puffy. What is happening with us?

We grabbed our things and walked into the house but I noticed the door was open. When I entered further everything was broken and some stuff like the TV was stolen.

"What happened here?" Tamika yelled.

I placed my hand over my heart and dropped to my knees because everything that mama built for us was destroyed. "I don't understand. I don't understand what's happening to our lives."

"Things'll be okay," Russo said helping me up.

"They won't!" I yelled. "They won't!"

Suddenly April came inside with Naverly. I had plans to drive her to a hotel later but now she could kick rocks or hit the streets again for all I cared. It was because of her my house had been broken into and now I was realizing it was dumb to let the bitch who stabbed me in the back into my house. Tamika was right.

So I ran up to her, snatched my daughter's hand and yelled, "GET OUT, APRIL! NOW! I SHOULD'VE NEVER LET YOU IN MY FUCKING HOUSE YOU STUPID, BITCH!"

She ran out crying.

"Bae, what you doing?" Russo asked, grabbing my free hand. "Why you just go on that girl like that?" He pointed at the door.

"How you sound? I told her to stay in this house with Naverly and now look! Everything my mother did was destroyed because she went out anyway!"

He took a deep breath. "Amina, Naverly called earlier when we were at Reggie's mom's house. She was hungry and I told them where the stash was for them to buy something to eat. That's why the girl left out. To grab some food. If you blame anybody pick me."

"Oh my, God." I flopped on the sofa and Naverly hugged my right while Tamika sat on my left.

"Don't worry about all that right now," he said. "Let me go get her right quick."

THE HOUSE THAT CRACK BUILT 2

I nodded and cried. "I feel like everything's breaking down around me." I said to Tamika. I totally overreacted but Reggie didn't tell me what he did earlier either. This is part his fault."

"We a mess out here right now."

I looked over at Naverly. "Go upstairs and play in your room. I'll be up in a second."

"Are you okay, mama?" She paused. "'Cause you look really mad with cousin April."

"I'm perfect, sweetheart. Now go upstairs. I want to talk to your auntie alone for a second."

She hugged me and then Tamika before taking off. "Amina, what's the real reason you having a hard time? Cause I know it's more than what you telling me."

I sighed. "Russo took Naverly out of here one day and got into a shoot out."

Tamika placed her hand over her mouth. "Oh no, Amina!"

"Exactly! And he didn't tell me. Naverly ended up bringing it up." I positioned myself so that I was looking into her eyes. "I love, Russo. More than anything. But I think he's got a darker side than I knew about. And...and I don't trust him. But I want to so much."

Tamika nodded. "I'm in the same boat as you. I feel like if I open my mouth I'm gonna start a fight but if I don't I'm letting him walk all over me."

"Did he say why he was staying over his mother's apartment?" I paused. "Because that's so weird. I understand him wanting to be with her because the world knows I miss mine but still..."

"No...and the worst part is, it's like he didn't care either." She paused. "He should've asked me and made sure I agreed before doing something like this. We never stay apart."

"With everything we got going on, 'Mika, the part I'm worried about the most is Drillo. I feel like maybe I should've did something more. That's why I don't want to throw April out so quickly. I figure if I do enough then things will be okay."

"Amina," April said walking into the house.

I wiped my face and walked over to her. "I'm sorry. About earlier and stuff. Just a lot going on."

Russo stuffed his hands into his back pocket and removed his keys. "We can't stay here tonight. Grab what you can hold and let's go. To my...I mean to the other house."

THE HOUSE THAT CRACK BUILT 2

RUSSO

I just tucked my daughter in bed and kissed her on the cheek. Normally she would drift right off but tonight her eyes were wide open, like she was trying to understand what was going on. "Sweet dreams, sweetheart."

I was about to walk out when, "Daddy."

"Yes."

"Can we stay here forever? Cause I like it better than grand mommy's house. It's not as nice as this one."

I walked up to her and kissed her on the cheek. "We'll stay for a little while. And then I'ma work on your mama to see if we can stay even longer than that."

She smiled brightly and I cut the night light on and went downstairs. I didn't blame my little girl. I didn't want to be there either but Amina was serious about not making a decision to be here a permanent one.

Tamika and April were in the kitchen laughing about something. But when I walked into the living room Amina was sitting on the couch, drinking brown, something she never did.

I sat next to her, put my arm behind her on the sofa and pulled her toward me. "It's gonna work out, Amina. I know it don't seem like it but shit always does for us."

"I know."

"Do you really?"

"Yes." She looked up at me. "But no more lies, Russo. About anything. I want us to be strong for each other but that means no more secrets. I can't take anymore."

"Trust me...we gonna be good and we already strong." I paused. "Can't nobody come in between what we got."

"Stronger than anything out there." She continued. "Not just when the doors closed. I mean we really have to trust one another above all."

I shook my head and laughed. "Wow."

"What?"

"Nothing, I just realized that after all these years I'm really a married man. I knew it but it's really sinking in right about now."

She sat up. "So you were out there fucking bitches the whole time and didn't realize I'm wearing your ring?"

"Wait...where the fuck that come from?"

"I don't know. That's why I'm asking you, Russo."

"I ain't mean it like that." I paused. "It's just that all this...the responsibility and shit like that. I never had to worry about stuff like this before I was married. And now...well...it's different."

She looked into my eyes. My wife is so fucking sexy and beautiful and sometimes I don't see it but now. Now with her sad eyes she's perfect. She's actually turning me on.

"Don't you love us anymore?" She asked.

"You know I do, Amina. Just as long as you remember who I am. And who runs this family. Okay?"

CHAPTER THIRTEEN

REGGIE

"**S**o you're leaving already?" Gina asked Reggie as he stood in the foyer of her new apartment. "You been at that hotel more than you been here." She paused. "I thought we would—"

"The boy said he wants to go home," Frank said sitting on the sofa, smoking a cigarette. "Let him."

Gina rotated her head toward her boyfriend and then smiled at Reggie. "I'm sorry about Frank," she whispered. "He's just anxious to break this place in that's all."

Reggie looked at Frank and pulled Gina closer to the door. "Ma, what's up with that dude for real? I mean, why you have him around you? He gives bad vibes off."

She sighed. "The truth?"

"Ma..."

"Because he makes me feel like I have somebody in my life who just loves me. Somebody who will be there when I wake up."

"I'm here too, ma. I just can't stay with you everyday all day."

THE HOUSE THAT CRACK BUILT 2

"I know and I don't mean to sound ungrateful but, I...never mind, son." She increased her height and kissed him on the cheek. *"I'll see you when you get back."*

He was about to leave when she tugged him a little. *"Oh, I hate to ask but..."*

He smiled. *"I meant to give you some money anyway."* He reached into his pocket and grabbed a wad of cash, handing it to her. *"Here. I'll give you some more later."*

She kissed him again and he walked out the door. The moment it closed her man got to plotting. *"You know, I got some niggas who would be willing to hit him over the head if he ever holds out."* Frank said. *"You know, fake like he don't wanna give up that paper no more."*

Gina rushed toward him. *"You stay away from him!"* She yelled. *"You hear me?"*

Frank rose up, backhanded her to the floor and helped her to her feet, only to take the money out of her hand. *"Watch how you come at me, Gina. Be very careful."* He walked toward the door, slamming it behind himself.

TAMIKA

Tamika pulled back the blind in the foyer of Russo's mansion to peer outside. When she saw her husband's blue Lexus pull up, she opened the door and ran outside. The moment his Jordan hit the pavement she jumped into his arms.

"Wow, somebody missed me a lot." He kissed her passionately. "But I missed you too."

"Then let's never do that again." She paused. "I hate rolling over and not having you in the bed with me. I barely got any sleep."

"I know, Tamika. It's not gonna be a regular thing. I promise. Just wanted to make sure my mother was settled."

"Never again, Reggie." She paused. "Since we started living together we slept together every night. And I know you upset that your mother and I couldn't get along but I...I need you here."

He exhaled, his minty breath tickling her nose. "Get in the car."

She ran around to the other side and slid inside, he did the same and took a deep breath before talking. "I'm not gonna lie, when my mother came back I had other intentions on the relationship I wanted her to have with you. Especially when I found out she was willing to get clean. And for whatever reason that's not going down the way I planned. But you right, we need to be there for each other."

"Whatever you want me to do I'll do. I'll even talk to her right now." *She paused.* "Want me to call her?"

He put his hand up. "No...don't do that. Besides, she has company. Just...just leave it alone, bae. Just let it be for right now okay?"

"So what can I do then?"

"Just chill, bae. I'm not the arguing type of nigga and maybe I didn't express that to you when we first got together but I'm doing it now. I prefer to let some shit go with the flow and to have fun more than all else. I dealt with enough hell in my life already. So can we do that?"

She took a deep breath. "Anything you want, Reggie. If you want a wife you can have fun with, I can be her."

He winked. "My type of girl." He looked at the front door. "So did we find out who robbed the house?"

Tamika shook her head no and looked down. "Nah, but can I be honest."

"What we just talk about?"

She laughed. "It's not about our relationship. It's about the house. After getting robbed and stuff I realize I don't wanna go back there. I like it here. I feel safe with the gates and I feel like, like royalty. It ain't like we don't know what Russo into with him being a drug—"

Reggie slammed his hand down over her mouth. "Never say more than need be."

She nodded. "I just want to stay here. Don't you?"

"Yeah. But we gotta go with the flow because I feel 'Mina on this shit too. She wants to stay closer to your mother and for her it's that apartment building or the house."

"I know. And I could do without both."

When the door opened and April stepped out he waved at her. She walked back in the house and closed the door. "So that's still going on too?" He asked.

"Yeah, but she's cool. I think—"

THE HOUSE THAT CRACK BUILT 2

"Hey, if you like it I love it." He paused. "But let's go inside. I'm hungry."

"I thought your mama was making breakfast."

He looked at her and tilted his head. "No shade."

They broke out laughing and walked inside.

Food covered the long mahogany table in the dining room. Russo and Reggie ordered takeout from Flemings Steakhouse and got more sides than their stomachs could hold.

Russo, Reggie, Amina, Tamika and April sat around the table drinking brown liquor, listening to music and laughing their faces off. But April decided to take it up a notch.

"Okay, let's play truth or dare!" She yelled. "And before you say anything just know that I'm not taking no for an answer."

"Nah, nah, nah," Russo contested, waving his hands from left to right. "The last thing I wanna do is get caught up in this type shit right here. I can already smell trouble."

"Why?" Amina asked. "It's just a game."

"For starters we drunk as fuck up in here," Russo continued. "And secondly we grown as fuck."

"And grown as fuck mean we can't play games?" Amina asked.

"Never said that," he responded pointing at her. "I just don't like games where shit comes out that's not supposed to when niggas are drinking that's all."

"Come on, Russo!" She paused, her voice swaying. "I'm bored and we need a little fun every now and again."

Russo looked around. "Everybody else okay with this?"

"Like I said, I ain't got no problems if you don't," Amina said. "Let's knock it out."

"I'm cool, too," Tamika added.

"Good," April said clapping her hands together. "Truth or Dare...uh..."

"Why do you get to start?" Tamika asked, frowning at her.

"Because it was my idea."

Tamika shrugged. "Proceed."

"Truth or dare, Tamika," she giggled. "Since you messed me up." She paused. "I dare you to kiss Russo."

"Nah, nah, nah," Russo said slapping the table with a firm hand. *"No kissing and shit like that. That's my sister."*

"It's just one little kiss," April persisted.

"Yeah, it's just one little kiss," Tamika responded.

Russo looked at Amina. "Fuck it," Amina said. *"You only live once."*

Tamika got out from her seat, walked toward Russo and planted a kiss on his lips. The problem wasn't the moment when their lips met, because rules were rules. What set Reggie off was when she inserted tongue and wrapped her arms around his neck.

"Fuck that shit!" Reggie got up from the table and slammed his fist on it before walking away. Tamika was right behind him.

"What's wrong?" She asked entering their room. *"Why you leave like that?"*

"Why I leave? What the fuck was that back there?" He pointed at the door before sliding out of his jeans. Next he removed his cell phone and tossed it on the bed. *"You played yourself like a whore. Like I'm not taking care of you in the bedroom or something so you gotta be freaked out."*

"What? I thought you wanted to have fun, Reggie." She said walking up to him. "Please don't be mad at me. I just wanted you to know I could be light if you wanted."

He laughed at her and walked into the bathroom, slamming the door behind himself.

The moment he left she sat on the edge of the bed and cried quietly. The liquor had gotten the best of her but she was also trying to show him that she could be a good time and now it blew up in her face in the worst way.

She was about to apologize to Amina, believing she was probably mad too when his phone rang. She picked it up from the bed and looked at the screen. The number was unknown.

Curious she answered it and heard a woman's voice. "Hello."

She was so shocked she hung up and dropped it on the bed before running out the room crying.

CHAPTER FOURTEEN

AMINA

Everybody in the house was asleep, I guess still hung over from the night before. For whatever reason I was up early, believing that with everything going on last night we could all use a big breakfast. And even though I wasn't mad at my sister about the kiss, because the shit was funny to me, I felt bad that she felt the need to beg for my forgiveness and that Reggie was so angry.

"Mommy, look what I got!" Naverly said happily. Before even looking at her I knew she'd gotten into my makeup again. Something she was famous for. But when I looked behind her I saw a stack of money. I quickly grabbed it from her, opened the kitchen drawer and put it back inside.

"Don't play with that."

"But—"

"You have all them toys in your chest!" I yelled. "Why you messing with daddy's stacks?"

"I'm sorry." She said softly walking away. "I was play shopping like you."

"Well you shouldn't be play shopping like me!" I yelled. "Crazy self." Why would Russo leave that amount of money lying around anyway? He always want people living here but does nothing to child proof the house.

I shook my head and continued to stir the eggs that included onions, green peppers and cheddar cheese, before checking on the bacon. When I turned the water on in the sink I thought I was hearing something crazy until I turned it off.

KNOCK. KNOCK. KNOCK.

I dried my hands and walked to the door. Slowly I opened it and immediately regretted my decision. A black man with albino skin and red hair stood in front of me. A huge black swastika sat on the right side of his face.

"Who are you?"

He laughed, his teeth the color of maple syrup.

"I SAID WHO THE FUCK ARE YOU?"

When I looked down I saw his yellow dick was in his hand and he was rock hard. "I'm gonna fuck your man hard with this, before I kill him."

I slammed the door in his face and could hear him laughing hysterically, his voice growing softer which meant he ran away.

"RUSSO! COME DOWN HERE NOW!"

I placed my hand over my heart and tried to calm my breathing but I couldn't stop. "RUSSO, COME DOWN HERE—"

"What is it, baby?" He asked wearing boxers, a gun in his grip. "What happened?"

"A man...a man was just here. He...he had a..."

"Where was he?"

"The back door."

"Where?"

"THE FUCKING BACK DOOR!"

He rushed to the door and bolted outside, the door swinging open. I saw him running barefoot left and right, gun aiming at nothing. Finally he re-entered out of breath and irritated.

"You promised we would be safe." I said, breathing heavily.

"I know." The gun was still swinging and he put it in the drawer before coming up to me to grab my shoulders. "We gonna be—"

I shook him off. "No! You promised. You fucking promised." I couldn't catch my breath and my thoughts seemed to crowd my mind. "And who was that...who was that person? Who was he?"

"Nobody. Just...just..."

"How did he get through the gates? How did he—"

"Amina, calm the fuck down!" He yelled. "Now I'm telling you it'll be okay. You see he's not here because there's no way he could make it through the gates."

"You lied and I want you to fix my house so I can go home."

"Okay, but it'll take a few days."

"I WANT TO FUCKING GO HOME!"

SLAP.

He hit me and I held the side of my face, unable to believe he had done what he did. I'm not going to lie, I always thought he was capable but now I had proof.

"I'm sorry, Amina."

"You hit me." The words came out in a whisper.

"I know and I'm begging you to forgive me."

"You fucking hit me."

THE HOUSE THAT CRACK BUILT 2

He took a deep breath. "Listen, I got excited and it messed me up. So please, please forgive me. But...but I..."

"Naverly, what's wrong?" I asked when I saw her standing in the corner. I now wondered how long she'd been there. "Baby, what's wrong with you?"

Instead of answering tears ran down her face.

"Honey, go back to your room so I can talk to your mommy. Okay?"

She shook her head no and I realized she had peed on herself, something she only did when she was scared. I ran up to her, gripped her up and ran her upstairs. When I heard him following I turned around and said, "Just leave me alone. Please."

When he stopped following us I took her to her room and cleaned her up.

I was cleaning the kitchen when Russo walked up to me. "I checked on Naverly. She was a little scared at first but I told her daddy's gonna protect her."

"Thank you." I exhaled. Not wanting to talk.

He took a deep breath. "You don't have to thank me. She's my daughter too."

"I know she is, Russo." I rubbed my throbbing temples. "I'm just...just spent right now."

He took a deep breath and held my hands. "Please forgive me. I know I was wrong but I just wanted you to calm down. I thought you would pass out the way you were breathing. But it'll never happen again. I promise."

"Okay. I forgive you...I just...I just need to think right now, I'm so sorry."

He hugged me. "Thank you so much for being easy going with this. I know it got you fucked up and it has me that way too. I appreciate you, Amina."

"For what?"

"For being in my life. Still."

"Yeah...I'm...I'm going to lay down for a moment." I smiled and walked away the entire time thinking how much I'm starting to hate his ass.

THE HOUSE THAT CRACK BUILT 2

CHAPTER FIFTEEN

TAMIKA

*T*amika looked across the other end of the Olympic sized pool at Reggie who was wearing a pair of goggles. "On your mark," she yelled, "Get set, go!" When she said that they took off toward the other end of the pool. Splashing water the entire way. "I beat, I beat!" Tamika yelled.

Reggie swam under the rope, grabbed her waist and hoisted her up in the air. She laughed hysterically before calming down as he looked into her eyes.

"I'm sorry, 'Mika." He paused. "I overreacted last night with the game and this right here, is a good idea."

She kissed him again, and slid her tongue into his mouth, grabbing a little unwanted attention by other swimmers. "I know you like swimming and—"

"You thought enough to bring me here." He paused. "I love you for this shit. With the summer being over I forgot all about being able to do this and...look."

"I hope you love me regardless."

"Always." He kissed her again, wrapping his arms around her waist. "But let me go pee right quick."

"So you don't pee in the pool like me?"

He frowned. "Fuck outta here with that shit!" He laughed as he crawled out, splashing drops of water in the process.

Wanting to go in the whirlpool at the recreation center, she slid out, grabbed her towel and walked toward the other side where the Jacuzzi was in the corner. Grabbing her book bag, which sat there, she heard a phone ringing. She reached inside, pulled it out and saw an unknown number again. Her heart pounded because with everything going on she forgot to question him about the girl's voice she heard on his cell. Plus she didn't want him thinking she was snooping. Especially with things going good.

"Hey, bae," Reggie walked up to her before winking. "You done with your laps?"

"Yeah, I wanted to warm up a little." She cleared her throat. "Your phone ringing."

He took it and said, "Oh, I left my towel in the locker. Let me grab it." He walked away with the phone, answered the call and put it against his ear.

THE HOUSE THAT CRACK BUILT 2

She turned around, stunned by his lies. She wasn't sure but she had an idea that the unknown caller was a woman, just like it was when she answered at the house. She was still thinking about it all when an older lady sat next to her.

"Beautiful day isn't it?"

Tamika nodded and tried to hold the tears back.

"Yeah, it's pretty," the older woman continued, answering for her. "Which makes me wonder why you're so sad. As pretty as you are I'd think the world is yours."

"No reason. I mean…I'm fine thank you."

"I'm a stranger who's willing to listen. Take advantage of the fact that you'll never hear from me again and tell me what's on your mind."

"I…it…"

"Can I guess?"

She shrugged.

"You're in love with a man who doesn't love you back."

"I hope that's not true." Tamika wiped away the tears sneaking up on her. "If it is I don't know what I'm going to do with myself. I don't…I don't know…"

"Well even if he does love you, if you can't feel it, isn't it the same thing?"

"Please, I just want to be alone."

"I'll leave you to it but let me say one more thing." She paused. "Now this isn't directed at you but it speaks to your age group these days. Young women get so caught up in wanting a man to love 'em, when they don't even know how to love themselves. How can you tell a man how to touch you, when you don't know what you like to feel? How can you tell a man how to treat you, when you don't even know what you like? How can you tell a man how to respect—,"

"I get it...and you're right." Tamika said irritated by it all. "But, maybe we smarter than you give us credit for."

"Meaning?"

"What if believing in the lie feels better than not having a man who'll care enough to do it? I know something's off, but I'd rather have it off than not have him around."

The old woman smiled. "Have a nice day, young lady." She eased out of the Jacuzzi just as Reggie was coming back.

He slid inside and placed his phone on a dry towel where he entered. "You look relaxed." He

THE HOUSE THAT CRACK BUILT 2

kissed her on the cheek and leaned back, closing his eyes as he took in the warmth and firm bubbles on his back.

"Feel good?"

"Yeah."

She bit her lip, drawing her own blood. "So, who were you talking too?"

"I wasn't talking to anybody."

Her heart thumped and when she looked across the recreation center she saw the old lady looking in her direction, as if mocking her. "I saw you get on the phone, Reggie." He opened his eyes and turned his head in her direction. "Please don't lie to me."

He sat up and moved closer. "Tamika, I'm not lying. I been in there for a minute because I had to...you know...take a dump. I forgot about the call I took when I first went in there."

"So who was she...I mean...who were you talking to on the phone? Just now. In the locker room."

"My mother." He looked into her eyes. "Why you asking?" He examined her for a while. "You okay? 'Cause you seem out of it a little."

She nodded. "I'm...I'm fine." He kissed her cheek again. "Was just asking that's all."

"Well I'm about to catch another lap before we leave. Maybe we can get something to eat from Bonefish." He paused. *"You hungry? Because I know I am."*

"Yeah. That'll be...nice."

He slid out of the Jacuzzi and got into the pool. Her eyes remained on him the entire time.

Reggie was in the locker room getting dressed when his phone rang again. When he answered it he was shocked to hear his mother's boyfriend's voice.

"I know you weren't expecting me but, I'm calling for your mother and it'll only take a minute."

Reggie sat on the bench in the locker room, expecting to hear the worst. "Why? Is everything okay?"

"Yes...I mean...you know she doesn't want to stay in your way and all because you have a family but she needs some more money. She was afraid to ask, thinking you would say no."

THE HOUSE THAT CRACK BUILT 2

Reggie scratched his head. "If she felt that way why you calling instead of her?"

"Like I said, man, she's scared." He paused. "You know how these females are out here. Scared to ask for what they want. Always needing a man to take charge.

Reggie tried desperately to contain his anger. "Put my mother on the phone, nigga," Reggie said through clenched teeth.

"Sure."

A minute passed before she came to the phone. "Hey...hey Reggie." The first thing he noticed was that it immediately sounded like she'd been crying. "Sorry to be calling you back, son."

"Ma, what's up? I just gave you some money."

"I know...but my asthma been bothering me again and I need another inhaler and stuff. I didn't want to say anything earlier because...you do so much for me already."

"Ma, are you sure you not...you know...using?"

"Never mind, son," she said. "I knew I shouldn't have bothered you."

"Wait!" He yelled. "I'll...I'll bring it over later."

"Really?" She said excitedly.

"Yes, but look, don't have that nigga call my phone about nothing no more. Now I know you

gotta have him how you gotta have him but, I don't trust him. Okay?"

"He's a really good man. He's just—"

"Are you hearing me, ma?"

"Yes, son. I'll see you later."

GINA

Frank stood over Gina with closed fists as she sat on the sofa. "How the fuck this little nigga gonna tell me not to call his phone?" He frowned. "I'm telling you he feeling himself right now."

He grabbed Gina's cell phone off the table and walked out the front door. "Hey, Ralph, I think it's time to get that nigga I was telling you about."

"You already know I'm with it." He chuckled once. "When you want to do it? Because I'm in need of a big payday."

"I'm gonna have the misses lure him here, and then I'll hit you when I'm ready."

CHAPTER SIXTEEN

AMINA

I knew something was wrong before he even came over to me. Before he even said a word. It was the perfect storm of events. First the man with the Nazi symbol on his face showed up at the door yesterday, and now Russo was huddled in the corner of his fancy living room, face against his luxurious wall paper, trying to hide his conversation.

I hate him so much right now.

When his call was over he walked toward me. It was as if he was moving in slow motion. "Let's go to the park." He looked at Naverly who was napping in my lap. Nudging her a little he said, "You wanna go to the park, sweetheart?"

As if she'd never closed her eyes she hopped out of my lap yelling, "YEAHHHHH!"

With perfect timing April walked into the living room and up to us. "Everything okay?"

"Yeah, we going to the park," I said slyly.

He cleared his throat. "Actually, April, you should come with us too."

That was all the answer I needed. Unlike the constant times he kept telling me I was safe I was anything but. It was obvious that even the wrought iron gate that surrounded this mansion couldn't keep us protected. We were being hunted.

He was on the phone again, some feet away from us. This time while Naverly played on the playground and April and me sat on the bench.

"I stabbed you," April said.

I looked at her crazily. "You trying to get me not to fuck with you no more?" I focused my attention back on Russo who was still heavy in conversation with someone.

"Nah...I'm very grateful actually." She paused. "Do you know how long I been wanting us to be friends again?"

"We're family. And if you really felt that way why you reminding me of something I'm trying to forget?"

THE HOUSE THAT CRACK BUILT 2

"I know why I'm here, Amina. You're smart, but I'm not dumb."

I adjusted myself so that I could look into her eyes. Suddenly my husband was no longer amusing. "What are you trying to say?"

"You invited me here hoping that I would come on to your husband and that you would have a way out."

I coughed. "What...that doesn't...what you..."

"It's okay, Amina. If you want me to come on to him I'll still do it. I'll corner him in the bathroom, drop to my knees and take him in my mouth before he has a chance to dispute. And it will work too. He fine enough, so it'll be easy. But what I won't do is go behind your back again."

My heart thumped in my chest. "I...I mean..."

"Look, I never got a chance to say it. As a matter of fact, I never said it at all. But I'm sorry for what I did to you, cuzo. I was in a bad place in my life. Living in a funky apartment, not having a parent to take care of me like you had with my aunt. And I...I guess Jordan just felt like an escape. But I regretted it the moment I first slept with him. And there is nothing, and I do mean nothing that will make me betray you again. You saved me. I was out in the streets and you saved me."

All I could do is hold my head down and laugh. "How did you know I wanted you to try him?"

"First off your mama was smart. And I know auntie didn't raise no dumb kids. It just didn't make sense that you would have me around after what I did to you without a reason. Still, people change, Amina. But that don't mean I won't be a soldier for you. If you need me to step to him I'll do it, or anybody else for that matter. Let me ride for you. You know I'm capable."

The more she talked the more I started to love her all over again. She was right, I did let her stay to see what was good with Russo. But he didn't look at her twice and she didn't look at him either. After awhile I just gave up.

"Yeah, I might need you for future shit but hold off for now."

"Say no more." She giggled. "But I will say this, Russo love you. Hard. But he a hood nigga and hood niggas got a different code."

"Meaning?"

"They live in the moment, Amina. He may react off cuff and not think about the impact 'til later. It don't mean he don't love you, it just means he's been born of a different breed."

I nodded. "The thing is I didn't sign up for all that."

"I hear you but tell the truth...do you really want another woman to step up and take your place?"

I thought about it and the idea of him being with anybody suddenly tasted like castor oil in my mouth. But what could I do with all the lies? They drove me crazy.

"Look, I'ma be honest, bae," Russo said before I could respond.

I adjusted myself. "We listening."

"You can't go back to my house or yours."

"Why, Russo? Is it cause of that man who showed up with his dick in his hand?"

"Yeah. And stop being smart."

I shook my head and laughed to myself. "But you said we would be safe. You said..." April nudged me softly out of view of Russo. "Never mind."

"Listen, I know you not feeling this. But give me some time to make a few moves to make us officially safe. Because whether you want to believe it or not, you in this for the long ride."

"There's always a way out."

"Not when you fucking with me."

There was no use in arguing. He had made his mind up way earlier in the day. That's why he had us leave the house and made it known we wouldn't be going back either.

If I wanted to be with Russo I had to strap up and take the long ride. Whatever that may be.

CHAPTER SEVENTEEN

AMINA

"So you gonna just act like you ain't got one card and didn't say Uno, bitch?" April said to Tamika as we all sat on the bed and played cards.

"I did say Uno." She yelled. "And stop cheating. You did that last time when I know I called it."

"Bitch, don't play with me." April said pointing a long finger in her face. "I been listening and when I play the tapes back in my mind your files are missing."

"Fuck does that mean?" Tamika asked as I giggled.

"It means you gotta draw four because you didn't call Uno."

"Ain't nobody drawing four!" Tamika said louder. "If I gotta do all that I ain't playing."

I stood up and said, "I'ma go get us some more soda while ya'll trying to figure it out." I looked over at Naverly who was sitting at the table coloring in her books. "Baby, you want some candy?"

She tossed the yellow crayon down and looked up at me with her big wide eyes. I never gave her candy or soda so this was a big moment. Opting instead of high PH balance water and fruit. But we were in crisis mode so I decided to give her a treat.

"Yes!"

"What kind?"

"Any kind, mommy!" She paused and grabbed my leg. "You always pick the best treats."

We all broke out into laughter. Probably because she ran game as hard as her father. "Okay, I got you. I'll be right back." I grabbed my wallet and walked out the door. On the way to the store I thought about how ironic it was that we had two homes and had to stay in a hotel to be safe. If this was a glimpse of my life man...I wasn't—

"Hey, sexy."

I turned around and almost dropped my wallet when I heard his voice. "Jordan. Is that you? What...what are you doing out here?"

He smiled. "Yeah...its me. Unless you met another nigga who looks like me and still misses you as much as I do."

THE HOUSE THAT CRACK BUILT 2

"My husband!" I blurted out. Embarrassed, I looked away but I could still feel him staring at me.

He laughed. "So your husband looks like me?"

"No...I mean...nah...I just thought you were trying to come on to me and...you know what...it doesn't matter. I'm just...it's been a long day and I'm just...talking I guess."

"So how you been?"

"Holding up mostly."

"What does that mean, Amina?" He paused. "Because I been wondering for a long time. Since you stopped taking my calls years ago."

"I stopped taking your calls because I wanted to move on with my life, after that thing with April."

He nodded. "Well, you should know that I'm sorry about all that. As fucked up as it is, it didn't mean that I didn't love you. And I know you don't believe me but, I...well...I'm sorry."

"You said that already."

"If I did I didn't mean it back then. But I mean it now."

I nodded, trying to get over how fine as fuck he looked. "So what changed?"

"For starters I found the Lord."

I rolled my eyes. "Jordan, don't play with me. I remember you saying that people who pray are waists of time. And now all of a sudden you gay for God?"

"I'm serious. The shit I used to do then I don't do now."

"And why is that?"

"Because ain't no future in it." He moved closer, and now I could smell his cologne. "And I had that with you. I'ma be honest, after you left me I thought couldn't nothing break me down but there's nothing like sitting in a room, alone, realizing you let a real one get away. The problem with that shit is niggas like me don't get a notice. There's no sign on women's faces saying, THIS IS THE SHAWTY OF YOUR DREAMS, BE CAREFUL WITH HER HEART."

"You would've still did you even if that happened." I shook my head. "For real the only reason I think you miss me is because I actually walked away and you never thought I would."

"Probably so. But not now. I'm grown."

I laughed. "Is that right?"

"Yeah." He paused. "Let me get your number, Amina."

"Nah."

THE HOUSE THAT CRACK BUILT 2

"Nah?"

"I can't...you too dangerous for my marriage."

"Danger is the prequel of serenity. You never heard that before?"

"Nah." For some reason that's all I could say.

"Well let me show you how that shit works."

I laughed. "I'm married."

"Like I give a fuck."

I giggled. "Thought you were a God fearing man?"

"Even God can't stand in the way of true love." He paused. "Besides, He the one who caused me to feel the way I do about you. I mean, what if you are with a man who is not a part of your destiny? What if you pushing the real man of your dreams away and you don't even know it?"

"Jordan, what we had was okay when I was young but—"

"First off you still young. Second of all here is my card. Tuck it away so you can put it in your phone when you get a chance. The moment that nigga fucks up, and he will fuck up, let me be the man you call. Because when I get my chance again I'm not letting it go." He walked off.

After he left I slowly walked to the store in the hotel and back to the room. With each step

Jordan was on my mind. The way he smelled. How he reminded me of when I was younger and when mama was alive. And how he looked at me. I been around the man a long time and he never, ever, looked at me like he did today.

When my phone rang I was nudged out of my thoughts. Looking down at the screen I saw it was my husband. "Hey."

"How my girls doing?" Russo said in a deep sexy voice.

"Ahn, uhn, nigga, I hear that extra base. You must be trying to get some pussy or something talking to me all sexy and shit."

He laughed hard. "I was that obvious."

"Yes!"

"Well you gotta forgive me because it's just that I miss you."

"Is that so?"

"Is that Russo?" My sister yelled in the background. "And is Reggie with him?"

"You heard her." I said to Russo with a smile on my face. The moment I heard his voice I remembered I was good in the man department. Fuck I need with Jordan when I was already with a winner?

"Tell her, her nigga right here. We about to—"

THE HOUSE THAT CRACK BUILT 2

BANG! BANG! BANG! BANG! Feet scuffling. Scurrying. Loud screaming.

"He been hit! My nigga been hit!" I heard a man yell. Except I didn't know whose voice it belonged to.

CHAPTER EIGHTEEN

AMINA

"Slow down, April!" Tamika yelled from the backseat as my cousin pushed the limits of my BMW. "I wanna make it alive to find out what's going on with Reggie."

"Drive faster!" I told April. And because we already had a conversation about her being my rider, she pushed the limits even harder on the car. Besides, we already dropped off Naverly to Mrs. Connelly's house so I wasn't about being squeamish. I wanted to make sure everything was okay at Russo's.

When we finally made it to Russo's mansion, the gate was open and at least twenty cars were parked in the driveway and his massive lawn. All of them had guns aimed at us until Russo told him who we were. He was sitting on the hood of a white Rolls Royce, his arm was getting bandaged up and his men surrounded him with shotguns.

I guess I knew who got hit.

My nigga.

I ran up to him, wrapped my arms around his neck and kissed his face several times. "It was you? Are you...are you okay? Did you...is it bad?"

"Yeah, but it just grazed me and is nothing serious." He paused. "But look, I gotta tell you something." He looked at his man who was wrapping his arm and he stopped bandaging him. Next we walked a few feet away from the crowd.

"What's going on, Russo? It looks like a crime scene out here without the cops."

"I found out who these niggas are." He touched my shoulder and looked deeply into my eyes.

"Well...who is it?" I asked seriously. "Because I can't have something bad happening to you, Russo. You don't know what I was going through when I thought I lost you."

"Bae, you remember them people who sold you the house?"

"You mean who you roughed it from? Wesley and his brother Peter?"

He nodded.

"Yeah...what about 'em?"

"They been wreaking havoc on us."

I backed up a little. "But I thought the dude who...raped my brother was dead."

"He is."

"So is he doing this as a ghost?"

"Nah, but his cousin is." He paused. "The dude with the Nazi sign on his face is his cousin. And I think the nigga who sold you the house is on some get back shit."

I felt like I wanted to throw up in my mouth. "So it's my fault all this been going on?"

"It ain't nobody fault."

"But...but...the shoot out when you were with Naverly...and the dude coming to the house...this was all because of me and having that house?"

"Look, I know you scared but—"

"I yelled at you. I yelled at you and..."

He grabbed my shoulders and looked into my eyes. "Listen, this is street shit. That means it's in my DNA so I'm built for it. Even if this didn't start from the house I still would have to deal with this. For real, now that I know it's about the house it makes me want us to stay there even more."

"Nah, I want it sold."

"How you sound? You don't give up on the war when somebody throw a grenade your way." I looked away from him. "Listen, Amina, one day someone will come along to lift Baltimore up. It's

THE HOUSE THAT CRACK BUILT 2

probably gonna be a female because it has to be someone with organization or heart. But when that day comes that property gonna be worth more than it ever was and I want our daughter to own a part of our history. So you can't sell it right now. Just move in here with me on a permanent basis. We can rent it out or something."

"I'm sorry."

"Don't be sorry, 'Mina. Be strong. There's a difference."

I nodded my head. "You're right."

He took a deep breath. "Now let me go see my niggas. We gotta discuss how to execute after this. But I want you to look around the yard. You see all these people?"

I laid eyes on all of them.

"They not leaving this property. And I like to see a nigga try some dumb shit now."

I nodded. "Okay, baby."

He kissed me deeply. "Let me go. I'll be right back."

I walked over to our porch and sat down just as Gina pulled up in a new truck. I figured Reggie and Russo took care of her as usual and now she had a ride. She walked up to me with a sad look on her face and the only thing I thought about was the fact that I didn't have time for any of it.

"Yes."

"I'm sorry about all of this."

I sighed. "Are you buttering me up because you can't find my sister?"

She placed her hands on her heart. "Wow. Is that what you think of me?"

I remained silent.

"Well I'm over here because this is a battle scene. And it makes me remember how important family is. And how much we really need to stick together." She took a deep breath. "I mean these are the trying times. Don't you agree?"

I remained silent.

"You seem tense?" She continued.

"Listen, bitch, right now I'm not in the fucking mood. My husband was just shot. Now I don't know why you coming at me like this because I never been the one, but let me set you straight right now. Back away."

She laughed. "You know what, you and Tamika are so pretentious."

"The big words huh?"

"When in the company of bougie bitches you have to flex."

THE HOUSE THAT CRACK BUILT 2

"And that's how you do it? By coming dangerously close to being slapped?"

"I wonder if you would say the same thing if you found out that your husband held your brother Drillo at gun point." She laughed. "Oh...you quiet now huh?"

"What you talking about?"

"All I heard from Reggie was that he wanted to get clean and Russo didn't trust him and threatened him to stay away. So the next time you think your world is so precious look at it from the other side. You'll feel differently."

She walked away and I looked across the field at Russo who was deep in conversation. He held a gun to my brother's head? He was troubled but he went that far?

I removed the card from my pocket and dialed. "Jordan. What you doing?"

"You, if you'll let me."

When Gina got back to her apartment building, she saw her male friend, Pigs was sitting in his car waiting on her. "Thank you for coming."

He laughed. "So now you need my help." He shook his head. "I was the reason you are back with your son but the moment you got him back you cut me off."

"I'm sorry, Pigs," she said. "It's just that things got away from me and—"

"You dumped me."

She sighed. "I know and I'm wrong too." She paused. "But I need you to do something major for me." She looked around and decided it would be best to slide in his car.

"What do you need from me now?"

"Earlier today my son was shot at but they hit somebody else instead." She looked for compassion from him and saw there was none there. "Well, the person who did it was Frank."

Now Pigs was interested. "You know this for sure?"

"Yes. I'm positive." She paused. "And I need you to help me get him. You do that, and you'll have me any way you want."

"I need more than that."

"Don't you hear me? I'll fuck, suck and give you anything you want, Pigs. No more paying me.

You been waiting on this for awhile and I'm telling you, that you'll have it."

CHAPTER NINETEEN

AMINA

Jordan was in front of the stove wearing only a pair of grey sweatpants and no shirt. He was searing two stakes in a skillet to trap in the juice before putting them in the oven. I had been here for three days and for three days straight he cooked breakfast, lunch and dinner for me.

A few times I woke up and he would be sleeping and I thought to myself, I can't believe I was in his bed without having to beg him. "Why you looking at me like that?" He asked giving me a large grin.

"What you think?"

"I think you 'bout to get some more of this dick if you keep staring at me like you crazy."

I laughed. "I can't mess with you anymore. My pussy still sore."

"And I'm not done." He opened the oven. "Get used to this because you're looking at your life."

I frowned a little. "What are you talking about?"

"I mean, since you chose me I—"

THE HOUSE THAT CRACK BUILT 2

"Jordan, I never said I would be with you exclusively. I said I didn't trust my husband and I needed a break and you said I could come to your house. That's why I'm here."

He walked over to me. "So you playing me?"

"No...I..."

"I have done everything I could to prove to you I care about you. I cooked for you—"

"But I didn't ask you to do that."

"I know you didn't, bitch."

My jaw dropped. I stood up and said, "You know what, maybe I should go home."

He ran in front of the door and blocked my exit. "You not going nowhere. We ain't spent enough time together. So basically I'm saying I have you and I need more."

"Jordan, move out the way." I tried to push past him and he stood in front of me again.

"Ain't you listening? I said you not going anywhere." He shoved me backwards and I fell on my butt.

I crawled toward the phone and he grabbed me by my hair. When I was on my back he stole me in my face three times and I felt my head wobbling. "Please just let me go, Jordan." Blood rolled down my throat. "I mean why are you doing this? I don't understand."

"Because you fucking played me, bitch!" He yelled, spit plopping on my face as he stood over me. "I did everything I could to prove to you I made a mistake. Cut that bitch off and everything."

"I just wanna go," I cried. "Please."

"Nah, I can't do that." He started pacing in large circles like he was seconds away from cracking mentally forever. "Because all you gonna do is go to the police and shit." He rushed to the back of the kitchen and returned with a gun. "I'm not going to jail for nothing, Amina."

My stomach started flipping and suddenly I realized this situation would not end well tonight. I did way too much and now I would have to pay."

I was in the bed with a man who had raped me for eighteen hours straight. And even though I begged him to stop he wouldn't. I was in so much pain every part of my body ached. My mouth. My pussy. My butt. My face. My limbs. Everything. All I knew was that I had to get out of here now or he would probably kill me.

"God, please help me," I whispered to myself. "I know I made things worse for my own self and I'm so sorry. All I wanna do is get back with my baby. Please."

Slowly I raised my head to look beyond the pillow I managed to lodge between us. When I did I noticed he was asleep and even snoring a little.

Okay, okay, so you have to move. I thought to myself.

Slowly I hung my left leg off the edge of the bed. Then I hung my right. When my feet were planted on the floor I slid out of bed and crawled on the carpet towards the door. I was almost out when I heard him yawn.

Instead of waiting I got up and ran as fast as I could.

"WHAT THE FUCK YOU DOING?" He yelled as he got up to chase me.

But there was no way I was going to let him catch me. This was my only escape.

Barefoot, with no purse and no money, I walked into a convenience store. Walking across the cold floor and up to the counter I leaned on it and said, "I need to use your phone."

"Ma'am, are you okay?"

"Yes...I...I..."

When I woke up I was in the hospital and surrounded by my family. "Baby, I thought I lost you," Russo said as he rushed up to me and wrapped his arms around my neck. "How do you feel?" He let me go. "Are you okay? Are you hurting?"

When I looked to my left Tamika was gripping my hand tightly and Reggie was behind her.

I looked back at my husband. "I'm...I'm fine."

"I know this is early but I need to know who grabbed you. Is this my fault? If it's my fault I gotta know now."

"It wasn't really your fault but..."

"Be honest, Amina. I let them niggas in our home and now they got to my wife. I'm telling you right now when I catch 'em its gonna be over. Believe that!"

I could've told the truth but why? It would only make things worse than they already were. So I decided to keep this secret to myself while praying it doesn't come back to me. Russo made some mistakes and I did too. Maybe I choose to believe we are now even.

CHAPTER TWENTY

TAMIKA

T amika ran up to Gina's door on a mission. Reggie hadn't come home the night before and she was beyond angry and irritated with how much he seemed to change. It was bad enough that her sister was raped and had gone missing but now...now her rock seemed to be elsewhere mentally. And when she asked where he was he said he was over his mother's house.

Once she made it to the door she took a deep breath and banged on it with a closed fist. But instead of the door meeting her knock it inched open. What she saw when she walked inside made her stomach churn.

Gina was in the middle of the floor with a stranger smoking drugs from a pipe. White clouds flew overhead and the room was heavy with the sweet, stinky odor of crack.

But what rocked her backward was the person she was getting high with. It was Pigs aka Peter, the man who sold the house to her mother when they first moved to Baltimore.

"What's going on?" She yelled as she entered.

THE HOUSE THAT CRACK BUILT 2

Both of them hopped up and scratched and paced in the center of the living room. "What are you doing in my house?" Gina asked, trying to look anything but high.

"I asked a question. What's going on in here?"

Peter laughed. "You have a nerve speaking to me. After what you did to my brother."

Tamika, clueless that Russo had done anything to his brother was confused. "I don't know what you're talking about." She looked around. "Where is my husband?"

"Get out of my house!" Gina yelled walking up to her. "Now! You're not welcome here!" She shoved Tamika out and slammed the door in her face.

Tamika ran out of the building and to her car, crying her eyes out with every step she made.

Tamika sat in her car talking to Reggie on the phone. "Reggie, I went to your mother's house and you weren't there...and...and she was using drugs...and...and..."

"Calm, down, Tamika."

"But, but she's...she's using and..."

"Bae, calm down and let me talk to you." He exhaled. "You must've came by after I already left. She was having some problems with some ex-drug addict and was thinking about using again. So I stayed over to try to talk her down."

"If that was true where are you now, Reggie?"

"The house." He paused. "Hold on, talk to April if you don't believe me."

"Hey, girl!" April said in the background.

"I don't want to talk to her. I don't want to talk to anybody. I just want to understand what I can do to make things the way they used to be."

He took a deep breath. "I'm going to say something to you but I don't want you to take it the wrong way."

"Go, go ahead," she sniffled, her eyes red and wild from hysteria. "I'm listening."

"We should've gotten you some help after that thing happened to you."

"So this is my fault?"

"Just listen to me, Tamika. We should have gotten you some help because you have been undone ever since you were raped. And I know the man's court case was this week and I also know

THE HOUSE THAT CRACK BUILT 2

you don't want to talk about it. Maybe that's why you leaning on me to do something I can't do right now."

"You mean loving me?"

"Of course not! I would never say that."

"Then I'm confused."

"Tamika, I can't make you feel comfortable every second of the day. I can't make you feel safe every second of the day either. But what I can do is be in your life and lift you up as much as you let me."

"Will you let that bitch who answered your phone lift you up?"

"What are you talking about?"

"The girl who keeps calling from the blocked number. I know about her, Reggie. I didn't say anything because you hate to talk about anything but now I don't care anymore."

"My mother calls sometimes from a blocked number but I—"

"I answered the phone, Reggie. The night we played truth or dare and I know it was a female."

"So you going through my stuff?"

"I hate you! I fucking hate you and whatever happens to me is your fault!"

Tamika ended the call and slammed the phone down. She drove erratically down the street as if she were about to kill herself. For some reason, like Amina, she was driven to go back to her old neighborhood. Reggie was right in some aspects. She definitely was trying to conceal the fact that she wasn't trying to deal with the court case and the man who raped her.

The prosecution called several times after learning that she was also a victim and each time she lied, saying she didn't remember what happened to her or that she never met him before. Tamika didn't want the weight of having to tell a room full of people what he'd done to her and what's worse, how.

It wasn't like she had peace.

Those details revisited her everyday while she was sleeping and it seemed to get worse every time. Nah, the last thing she wanted was to talk about that night but what she decided to do was prove to herself that she wasn't afraid anymore, even if it didn't make any sense. Which is why she decided to revisit the building.

When she pulled up to the block, where she was raped, ironically the same parking space was available for her that the van was parked in some years back. Just being there caused her skin to crawl and she was so ill that she opened the door, stuck out her head and vomited on the concrete.

When she was done she realized how stupid the idea was and that maybe Reggie was right, maybe she did need help. She decided to get some more information on rape counseling and then she saw her brother, Drillo, standing at the passenger's side door.

"Can I get in?" He asked.

CHAPTER TWENTY-ONE

AMINA

Today was my first day out since I'd been home a few days ago from the hospital and it was hard getting Russo to let me go alone too. Even when he finally said yes I saw one of his soldiers driving behind me, trailing me and watching my every move.

All I wanted to do was get my hair done, relax after a sweedish massage and go to the pharmacy. I realize the things don't go together but they had to in my case. Because I found out today that Jordan gave me Gonorrhea. Luckily I was able to resist Russo sexually by saying it was too soon to make love after being raped but I didn't know how much longer I'd be able to do that either.

When I walked through the doors of Russo's mansion, my prescription in my purse, I smelled the scent of food cooking and my stomach rumbled. "Wow, what is Rosa making?"

Russo walked up to me, removed my purse and sat it on the table. "Hey, bae. How you feel?"

"I'm not sick, Russo."

THE HOUSE THAT CRACK BUILT 2

"I know but, I still wanna...check on you."

"MOMMMMMMY," Naverly said running up to me. I lifted her up and kissed her cheek. "You not gonna leave again today are you? I don't want you to go back to the hospital."

"No, baby. Of course not." I kissed her again and put her down. "Mommy's good." I looked around. "But what is Rosa cooking?"

"A little bit of everything. Just for you." He said as we walked to the dining room.

Some hours later, Russo walked back downstairs after tucking Naverly in for a nap. When he was done he sat next to me and looked into my eyes. "That shit was good wasn't it?"

"You mean Rosa's skillful ass in the kitchen?" I giggled. "Because she's Chef Bae."

"Tell me about it." He chuckled again and then grew serious. It was like I was looking at a totally different person. "You got something to tell me...wifey?" He asked through clenched teeth. "Something I wanna hear from your own mouth?"

"What...what you talking about." Suddenly the seat was uncomfortable.

"I know, Amina. I know where you been."

My heart thumped so hard that when I looked down I could see my chains moving up and down on my chest as I battled with my breath. "I was at the—"

"Bitch, you were with that nigga Jordan!" He said through clenched teeth.

"No I wasn't!" I stood up because I could feel a slap coming on and I didn't want to absorb how painful I knew it would be. "If he saying it he's..."

Suddenly he removed his phone and showed a video of me I didn't know Jordan took. I was lying on my back, and he was fingering my pussy while I was moaning. Not only was it evident that I was enjoying it, it was also evident that I was drunk.

Caught red handed, I took a deep breath and stood up. "You right. I did—"

He gripped me up, slapped me down and helped me to my feet for another slap. "This nigga got in contact with my people and then sent this to me! After the whole neighborhood saw it!" He puffed. "So you telling me I gave my ring to a slut? I had a child with a bitch who ain't no different then the rest of these birds out here on the streets?"

I held my cheek, the pain in my heart overcoming the pain on my face. "You said you wouldn't hit me again."

"And you promised to be faithful, in good or bad and you lied to me!"

I couldn't understand the rage welling up in me but it was great. So great that my nostrils flared as I looked at him. "Yeah I fucked another nigga, and you put a gun to my brother's head and threatened to kill him!"

The rage diminished from his face a little. "So you telling me you stepped out on our marriage because I kept an addict out of our family? That's what you saying?"

"He's my brother!"

He paced where he was and stomped toward me. "You not about to change shit around on me this time. You a bird, bitch. And even if we get past this our shit will never be the same."

"It was never the same the moment you started lying to me."

"Lying to you? When the fuck I do that?"

"You promised to have the house fixed up and—" He broke out into laughter. "Fuck so funny? I asked.

"I'm the one who paid to have that bitch, ransacked. Why would I fix it up?" He laughed harder. "But don't worry, I'ma have that piece of shit fixed so you can move into it. But my daughter, she staying here."

My eyes widened. "I'm not leaving without my daughter."

"And what you gonna do? You don't know the nigga you married if you think I'ma sit by and let you put her in harms way."

I stepped back and looked at him harder. "I don't know you."

"You couldn't have if you thought I would let you pull some stupid shit. She staying right here in this house."

"I hate you!"

"I fucking hate you too, bitch!" He stomped toward the door. "And I got my people still watching my crib. If you take her outta here they got orders to drop you at the door." He pointed at me. "So don't try nothing." He stormed out.

Fuck him. I'm leaving and taking my baby outta here. I don't care what he said. I was about

THE HOUSE THAT CRACK BUILT 2

to put my plans into action as I stomped up the stairs when I saw one of his men guarding the door. I felt gut punched. He really had someone watching us in our own home.

"I'm taking my daughter and leaving." Suddenly the door opened and a female walked out.

"Oh...hey," she smiled. She was uncomfortably beautiful and my stomach churned again.

"Who the fuck are you?" I asked stepping to her.

"A friend of Russo's. And don't worry about your daughter. She's sleep. But you can go wherever you want though." She looked at one of Russo's men. "We got it from here."

GINA

"Okay, he's coming now," Gina whispered to Pigs who was hiding in her bedroom waiting on Frank who was walking up the steps of the

building. "You got the bat right? And you gonna hit him the moment he comes inside right?"

"Yeah, now close the door."

"I wish you had a gun instead. This way is so bloody."

"Gina, close the G Damn door!"

When she closed it she turned around only to see Frank standing in front of her. "Who you talking too?" He asked suspiciously.

"Nobody..." she smiled. "I was just excited about you coming up and all."

"But I thought you were still mad at me, for the attempt on your son."

"Why would I be mad?" She paused. "You got his friend instead. I didn't give a fuck about him." She shrugged. "Now let's—"

"Get off me woman," he said shoving her for the bedroom door. When he opened it he was shocked to see Pigs waiting with a bat. Instead of being afraid he laughed and walked up to him. "So you think you gonna do something to me? You think you man enough?"

"No...I..." Pigs backed into the wall, afraid to confront the man one on one. "I was just...Gina made me do it."

THE HOUSE THAT CRACK BUILT 2

Frank stopped in his tracks. "She did, did she?" He turned around and hit Gina with a closed fist before charging after Pigs, snatching the bat from him and beating him hysterically with it.

When Gina tried to help after coming too, he dropped the bloody bat and backhanded her back down. It was time to kill her. So he raised his shirt, and released the revolver he never left home without. He was about to shoot her when Pigs used the strength he had to pull himself up and hit him in the back of the head.

Once Frank was on the floor Gina grabbed the gun and shot him in the middle of the forehead.

"Now we gotta get rid of this body," She said.

CHAPTER TWENTY-TWO

RUSSO

Reggie and me were cruising down the street on our way to the shop. When I looked over at him he was deep in thought. I fucked with him but I'm not gonna lie, I wasn't feeling him telling my wife about our little situation with Drillo. Especially if that caused her to step out on our thing.

"Can I trust you?" I asked him.

He nodded. "You already know the answer to that. Why even come at me this way?"

"Do I know the answer? Really? Because to tell you the truth, I'm definitely confused."

"Okay." He sat his phone down in his lap. "I'll play along. Where this coming from?"

"Did you tell Amina about Drillo?"

"Fuck no!" He yelled. "Shit already shaky at the house. What I look like adding to it?"

I scratched my head and continued to steer down the street. "Then how the fuck she find out?" I said mainly to myself.

"Awww...fuck!" He said. "No, no, no, no!"

I looked over at him. "What?"

THE HOUSE THAT CRACK BUILT 2

"I didn't tell her but I was talking to my mother about it right after it happened. When I was helping her with her new place and shit."

"What the fuck? Why, yo?"

"I don't know, man. I was drinking and venting I guess." He threw his hands up and let them fall back in his lap. "I'm trying to figure out when she would even have a chance to tell Amina."

"She was there the night I was shot." I shook my head. "Now that I think about it, I saw her rapping to her but figured it was something lightweight. But now..."

"Sorry, man. I didn't know she was going to do any of this shit. For real."

"What's going on with her and the wifey anyway? Because from where I'm standing it don't look like shit is gonna change. Ever."

He shook his head and ran his hand down his face. "Man, she hit me about my mother supposedly being on drugs and..."

"Wait...So you still don't know?"

"Know what?"

"Yo, I thought you were already aware of that shit, Reg. The streets been talking. Your moms definitely been back at it. Hard too. I already told my niggas not to fuck with her but you know...that ain't gonna stop her from getting at it if she want it."

Reggie shook his head and threw his head in the headrest. I could tell that he honestly had no idea. "What am I gonna do?"

"It ain't a lot to it. You gonna have to ride with the wife or lose everything." I paused. "And how that situation going?"

"I been calling Tamika for ten hours straight and nothing. I think she stopped answering my calls. Yeah I been staying at hotels to relax and get away from the drama but that's it." He paused. "She think I'm fucking with some bird but I found out moms must've had somebody in her building call me from a blocked number just to fuck with her." He paused. "'Cause on mother's the last thing I'm doing out here is messing with another female."

Just when he said that my phone rang and I looked down at it. "On that note, I'ma drop you off at the shop. I gotta hit this female real quick."

Reggie shook his head. "I don't wanna know nothing." He dapped me up and I pulled in front of the spot.

THE HOUSE THAT CRACK BUILT 2

When he was gone I met Tamara at the address she gave me. She slid in my car and we pulled up in an alley. "Wait, where we going?" She asked.

"You said you wanted to do it anywhere." I looked around. "This looks like just as good a place as any." I undid my pants.

"But I wanted to—"

"Oh you playing games." I zipped my pants back and threw my car into drive. "Let me take you to—"

"Wait!" She yelled. "I'ma do it."

"Then why you talking instead of sucking?" I paused. "Time is important to me right now and you taking too much of it."

"You right," she undid my pants again pulled out my man and went to work.

Her warm mouth made me immediately relaxed and not worrying about my problems. But then every time I tried to get really good into it the vision of my wife getting off on another nigga entered my mind. She may have been mad at me but she went too far to seek revenge. It made me wonder what else she would do.

Trying to put my mind back onto the situation at hand, I look down and pumped into Tamara's mouth. She took it all, allowing the shaft to rest in her throat.

"Keep doing that shit just like that."

"You like it?" She smiled.

"I love it."

For five minutes she sucked me off with precision and when she was done my nut rolled down her throat. "Damn, that shit was right." I zipped my pants.

She wiped the corners of her mouth with her fingers. "I do a good job?"

"You drank milk right?"

She giggled. "I guess I did." She put her hand on my chest. "So you taking me to get something to eat?"

I laughed. "What about this situation made you think we going public?"

"But...I...I mean."

"What?" I paused. "You said, and I quote, I'm just trying to suck you right. It'll only take a few minutes."

"But I wanted..."

"Look, I'm married. You already knew that so I don't even see why you being brand new right now."

I was about to pull off when she slapped me with her nails. I could feel my skin opening up under the blow and lost it. Grabbing my gun from the glove compartment I pulled it out, aimed at her and shot her in the hand. Then I ran around to the passenger's side and pulled her ass out.

"Stupid, bitch!" I yelled as I got into my car and pulled off. "FUCK!"

CHAPTER TWENTY-THREE
REGGIE

*I*t had been three days since Reggie had spoken to Tamika and he wasn't the only one concerned about her whereabouts. Amina, who was already stressed out that her marriage was probably broken forever and that Russo felt it necessary to bring people in the house to prevent her from removing her own daughter, was also worried. Tamika going missing too caused her stress and had even made Russo meaner. If it wasn't for April being on hand to be an ear to those who wanted to vent, they probably would've killed each other.

Reggie was still spinning his wheels and driving up and down the streets to find Tamika when Mrs. Connelly said he saw her walking toward the house in Baltimore earlier that day. Relieved, he quickly made a U-turn and drove to the house. He was one block away when he saw Tamika holding grocery bags.

"Get in, Tamika," he said as he rolled the window down.

She looked at him, rolled her eyes and kept moving. "Nah, I'm good."

He pulled over haphazardly, jumped out and lifted her up. "Get the fuck off me!" She yelled as if a stranger was kidnapping her. When he tucked her in the seat he ran to the other side but she got out again.

"Fuck!" He yelled until he finally caught up to her, tackling her to the ground. "What is wrong with you?" He maintained a tight grip on her arm.

"Why do you care?" He stood up and helped her up too. She maintained control of the bags in her hand.

"Bae, you been gone for three days. Haven't been answering my phone calls and now I find out you back here. What is wrong?"

"What's wrong is everything. I trusted you to take care of me and to love me and what do you do? Hurt me even more. I can't deal with you and your mother. I'm done."

"Alright!" I yelled.

"Alright what, Reggie?"

"Alright I'll...I'll take hands off my mother unless she's clean." He walked a few feet away and sat on the hood of the car. "Come here, yo." He extended his hand and she slowly walked over

to him and accepted. "I know I been giving you the blues lately but, but I wanted...I wanted you to know that...that..."

"Maybe I was wrong," Tamika said softly.

"About?"

"I mean, I know you love your mother and I know you want only the best for her. And maybe I was wrong about you not giving your all to save her."

"Bae, I'm confused."

"Why?" She paused. "I'm being as clear as possible. Maybe I made a mistake. She's your mother and—"

"If you feel that way then why aren't you back home? Why I have to find our from Mrs. Connelly where you are?" He asked putting his hand on his chest. "Do you know how bad I've been lately? Do you know how crazy I've made myself when I roll over only to find that you not in the bed with me? If you wanted to get back at me it's working."

"I know. I just needed to get away."

"Well you need to come back now." He looked over her and at the house. "I mean, why are you even staying here? It's trashed."

"I cleaned it up a little. It's not like it used to be but it'll do."

THE HOUSE THAT CRACK BUILT 2

He looked down at the groceries in her hand. "Look like you planning to stay here for awhile too." He touched her face. "Come back with me. Let me draw you a bath, clean you up and show you how much you mean to me."

She smiled a little. "Okay...on one condition."

"Anything, 'Mika."

"That you let me stay here alone tonight. I promise I'll be back home tomorrow."

He frowned. "But why you wanna even be here? It's nasty, Tamika. And you look like you haven't had a bath in months. Come with me now and—"

"Respect me now or leave me alone!" She yelled.

He looked her over slowly. "All right...alright." He stood up straight. "I'll leave you here tonight but I'll be back tomorrow if you aren't home by then. I'm sorry but I'm already not feeling good by leaving you here so you'll have to accept."

"Okay." She smiled.

"Let me take the bags to the—"

"I got them, Reggie." She grabbed them from him. "I'll see you tomorrow. Go home and get ready for me." He was about to pull off when she yelled, "Can I have some money?"

"What...for what?" He paused. "You gonna be home tomorrow."

"Please."

He dug into his pocket, handing her two hundred dollars. "Thank you."

"Yeah, aight." He pointed at her. "But remember, I'll be back here in the am if you not home when I roll over."

"You got it." She smiled before watching him ease slowly into his car and pull off, driving down the street.

When he was gone she walked into the house where Drillo was sitting on the couch watching a TV that used to be in Amina's room. "You got the food." He rubbed his stomach. "Because I'm hungry."

"Yep!" She smiled. "Stole it right off some lady's cart when she was getting her car." She paused. "But we don't have to sell it now. I ran into Reggie and he gave me two hundred dollars!"

She and Drillo jumped up and down happily. "More than enough to buy some more drugs."

Tamika tossed the food on the couch and she and Drillo walked out to score. An outsider looking in would probably say the house turned all those who were not strong enough and lived within its *wall to fiends, and they may be correct. Because already it had claimed the souls of two young people, brother and sister.*

CHAPTER TWENTY-FOUR

AMINA

Russo and me hadn't said two words to each other since we got into that fight and to be honest I was tired of it. Although soldiers were still outside he stopped them from coming into the house after I begged him and promised not to remove Naverly. He didn't tell me what he was going to do either, but I was glad that he respected my wishes.

When he came home after two more days of silence I was waiting on him. "I'm sorry."

"About?" He walked past me and into the living room. "Because I'ma be honest, I'm not in the mood today."

"About fucking another man when I knew I was married. I let my emotions get in the way and—"

"Be careful with the words you use to describe your little situation." He paused and cracked his knuckles and glared at me. "That shit still got me raw and I got people out looking for your mans right now as we speak."

I sat next to him. "I know and I'm sorry, Russo." I took a deep breath. "I really am even though you may not believe me. I'm even sorry that you standing up for me with that house when my mother was alive is the reason you got drama in the streets right now. I want peace and I don't want to argue with you anymore but you have to do something about your temper if we are going to stay together too. You hit me more than enough times and you held a gun to my brother's head when you know how much I love him."

He took a deep breath. "I may have been wrong. You know what...on second thought I was wrong about that part. But...you don't know how much I care about you. That video sent me off the ledge, Amina. Don't you understand what type of shit a nigga like me is capable of? Don't you know how many people I would be willing to destroy if it meant keeping my family together?"

"I get that but we can't keep doing each other like this." I paused. "You getting angry with me and lashing out violently. And me fighting with you or...or stepping out of our marriage. I want to know we can really work otherwise, if we can't, maybe we shouldn't be together."

He laughed. "And where would you go, Amina? Back to that crack house you tried to make a home?"

"The way I feel I would go anywhere, Russo." I paused. "I may even move out of state."

"Even if it meant you couldn't take Naverly with you?" He asked with lowered eyes. "Because I'm serous about one thing. There is no way I can see you taking her out of this house, especially with everything going on out here in the streets."

"I love her more than I even knew was possible, Russo. And I want her with me. And, I can honestly say I understand what my mother meant when she said she'd do anything for us, even if it meant her life." I took a deep breath. "But, I know the hate you have in your heart right now is geared toward me and not our child. And that makes me feel like leaving her with her father would still allow her to be safe. So that's what I would do since I don't have a choice. I'd just have to stay on my knees every night so she'd know I never meant to leave her. And after that I will go because I will never allow you to hit me again. Ever, Russo." I paused. "Do you want me to do that?"

He sighed and sat back in the sofa. "No...I...you know that's not what I see for us. Otherwise you wouldn't be here."

"Then what do you want?" I pleaded, putting my hand over my heart. "Tell me what I gotta do."

"Right now I don't want anything but a clear mind." He paused. "And I don't have that right now do I?"

"Do you blame me?"

"I don't know who I blame."

"Russo, what can I do to put us back together? Because you not answering the question." I asked softly. "Anything, just let me know."

"You already said you wouldn't give me anything remember? Said if I hit you again you'd be out."

"So you want me to let you hit me to stay?" I asked, tears rolling down my cheek.

"No...of course not..." he stood up. "I'm just—"

"Let's pray together, Russo. I know you don't believe in all of that but I do. And when I stopped dropping to my knees and asking for help things started falling apart in my life. Maybe you can pray with me."

He looked away. "I got niggas trying to take off my head and you want me on my knees?" He asked through clenched teeth.

"If they are successful, in taking your life, won't you be glad you did?"

He sat down and I slid on my knees. "I can't...go lower than I am now but I'll...I'll be here while you pray."

I smiled. "Okay...that's a start."

I closed my eyes and said, "God, I know—"

"I just heard some fucked up news about Tamika!" Reggie said running into the living room. "We have to get over to that house! Now!"

When we walked to the house and opened the door I couldn't believe my eyes. Drillo was sitting on the floor, in the corner of the living room nodding off and Tamika was on her knees throwing up in the loveseat as if it were a toilet. I felt like someone walked up behind me and hit me in the back of the head with a bat.

She looked up at us, her face almost grey, and passed out. Reggie rushed up to her, picked her up and ran her upstairs. Russo and me followed.

CHAPTER TWENTY-FIVE

TAMIKA

S ome hours later, after going to the doctor's, Tamika sat in a tub of lukewarm water, her right cheek on her knees, which were drawn closely to her body, her eyes resting on him. "Thank you for all of this...and I'm sorry."

"Don't be sorry," he said softly, his eyes filling up with tears. "I failed you."

"Why...why do you say that?"

"I made a promise to your mother and I made a vow to you and both were broken just because...I wanted to be there for a my moms. A woman who gave up on me a long time ago."

"Let's not talk about that anymore. It hurts too much."

"Nah, we do too much of that as is, Tamika." He said passionately. "What made you take this route? Is it Drillo?"

"No...it's not him." She took a deep breath. "At first I was doing it for revenge. It seemed like everywhere I turned drugs were messing up the situation I had with my family. First with my brother and then with you with your mother. I

THE HOUSE THAT CRACK BUILT 2

guess I wanted to see what all the hype was about. I wanted to see was it worth it and if I was strong enough."

"Was it worth it?"

She smiled. "At first it was. It was like every problem I ever had in my life suddenly became meaningless. I felt happier and more in touch with the earth than I ever had been. And then it wore off, and I felt dirty, angry, anxious and unhappy."

"Tamika, this...this is fucking me up." He rubbed his head. "I never wanted this for you."

"And I never wanted it for myself." She sat up. "What is my sister saying?"

"She's not happy about none of this shit. I can tell you that." He paused. "But I know you know that already."

"What about Russo?"

"He trying to find the niggas who sold to you." He paused. "You know how he is. He don't care about all the steps in between. He just be wanting to get to the person at the end."

"I hope nobody will get hurt."

"I can't make any promises."

She sighed deeply. "I know." She paused. "Now what?"

"For starters your sister is still trying to figure out what's up with Drillo. He said he would hang around because he was worried about you but he bolted when we went downstairs to question him."

"He told me about what Russo did to him." She said. "By putting a gun to his head."

Reggie looked away. "Did he?"

"Yes, and I don't want him hurt."

"Tamika, I'm done worrying about what happens to other niggas. I know it's wrong and I know you may think I'm heartless but my wife is sitting in a tub of cold water after almost overdosing. My head was all over the planet when it came to you but not anymore. I'm focused. And all I want is to make sure you aren't hurt anymore."

KNOCK. KNOCK. KNOCK.

The door opened and Amina walked inside. Reggie stood up and said, "I'ma leave you two alone. Call me if you need me." He walked away, closing the door behind himself.

"He really, really loves you," she sat on the floor and turned the warm water on. "You're lucky."

"I know what you're about to say, sis."

THE HOUSE THAT CRACK BUILT 2

"Do you?" Amina said softly. "Because I have no idea what I'm going to say to this. What were you thinking?"

"I don't know." She shrugged.

"That's not good enough, Tamika."

"And you haven't made some mistakes recently?" Tamika asked. "When April was here earlier she made a mistake about mentioning your situation with Jordan."

Amina rolled her eyes. "Yeah, she wasn't happy about it when I told her we slept together again either. I don't know if she was mad because I was fucking up a good thing with Russo or if she still has feelings for Jordan."

"April's cool." Tamika shrugged. "Cooler than I suspected her to be anyway."

Amina sighed. "Yeah, I know."

"What am I going to do?" Tamika asked. "I don't want to be an addict. I don't want to be like Drillo. Having to borrow or steal from my own family to support my habit." Tears rolled down her cheeks. "I actually had my husband give me money for drugs and I have been feeling worthless ever since."

Amina crawled closer and grabbed Tamika's face. "This shit will not take you too."

"You can't say that. What if—"

Amina grabbed her face harder. "This shit will not take you too. Do you hear what I'm saying? It took Drillo and it almost took your husband because of his mother. We gotta fight this shit and we can."

"Do you really believe that?"

"Yes...I really, really do." Amina released her. "Russo wants me to sell this house."

"Are you?"

"I don't know." She exhaled. "Me and him going through some stuff right now. I think we gonna try and work on it but I can't give up our safe haven, only to realize we won't be able to work on our marriage and have no place to go." Amina looked around. "And I know it's stupid but mama wanted us to have this house so badly. It would be a shame to throw it away."

"But Reggie says the house is cursed."

"Houses don't curse...people do." Amina paused. "So maybe we can turn it around if we live happily here."

"Maybe."

Amina took a deep breath. "Now let's get you out of here. We have a lot of work to do."

THE HOUSE THAT CRACK BUILT 2

"*Actually you mind if I sit here a little longer? By myself.*"

Amina smiled. "Nah, I'll be downstairs."

When she left Tamika jumped out of the tub, her wet feet slapping against the floor. After locking the door, she removed one of the six stacks of toilet tissue sitting on the shelf, she tapped it once and a bag of crack, her drug of choice, fell in her hand. She threw on her robe and put it carefully in her pocket.

"*Just one more hit and I'll stop, mama.*" *She whispered to herself. "I promise."*

CHAPTER TWENTY-SIX

RUSSO

When Reggie came downstairs I tucked my phone in my pocket and rushed up to him. "They found the black Nazi at some broad's house. We have to go now."

"Let me get my gun." Reggie said before dipping toward his jacket that sat over the edge of the couch.

When he was done we ran out the door but when I turned around Amina was grabbing my hand. "What's going on? Where you going?"

"I gotta make a few runs." I paused. "But get your sister out of here and take her to my place."

"But we need help." She said. "Are you taking Reggie? Because I can't get Tamika downstairs without him. And April still at the house with Naverly."

Fuck! Fuck! Fuck!

I walked over to Reggie. "Okay, you stay here with the girls." I said to him.

"Are you sure 'bout this, yo? Maybe we should do that another time."

"Positive." I paused. "Just make sure the girls are good. I'ma take care of this." I jumped in the car and peeled out.

I saw the Black Nazi standing on the side of a house smoking a cigarette. He was wearing black shorts and a black wifebeater. Behind me were three of my men all loaded and ready for everything that came our way. I was ready and eager for this shit to be done with once and for all.

As I looked at him my jaw twitched. This nigga had been causing problems for me for a minute and I had plans to take him out tonight.

"Ya'll get ready," I whispered.

"We need to—"

The first bullet went through my friends' head, his blood splattering on my face. The second and third took care of my other soldiers.

And the fifth and sixth....

AMINA

I was sitting in the kitchen drinking wine with April thinking about everything. "You don't look too good," she said as she sat next to me, grabbing a slice of cheddar cheese along with a cracker from the tray. "What's on your mind?"

"How do you know I'm thinking of something?"

"I can tell."

"Speaking of can tell I like how you told Tamika about Jordan." I rolled my eyes. "Please don't tell me you're still sweet on him. Because that would be a mistake. The man is crazy."

She laughed. "To be honest I haven't thought about him much since I moved here. The only reason I thought about him before that was because I blamed him for my situation. But now..."

"Now what?"

"Now I'm realizing I was a willing participant." She sighed. "Jordan was an escape, like I told you and he was convenient for me when it was good but that was it."

I shook my head. "Yeah, I get that."

"So what's on your mind?"

I sighed deeply, drinking the rest of the wine in my glass. "I don't feel good about the next chapter of my life."

"Chapter?"

"Yep." I looked at April seriously. "It's like this...the first chapter was when I was born, the second and third were me growing up and getting a boyfriend and the fifth was meeting Russo before later becoming his wife. What if the chapter after this changes everything as I know it?"

"You think he's gonna get hurt today?"

"I feel like he already has."

She frowned. "I'm confused. I never knew you to be a mystic or anything like that."

"And I'm not now...I just feel like this day is my last like this." I took a deep breath. "Maybe I should cherish it. Remember the chaotic peace as I call it before it gets worse."

Reggie came running toward us. "Come with me. I think Tamika is using again."

My eyes widened. "In this house?"

He nodded yes and the three of us followed him.

When we walked into Tamika's room she was moving erratically in the middle of the floor. "What...what's wrong with ya'll?"

I walked toward her and could tell right away she'd been smoking. Please God don't let this be our life. "How 'bout you tell me what's going on? You looking kind of crazy right now."

She wiped her nose erratically and tried to place her hands under her pits but it was like she couldn't get comfortable. "Ain't nothing wrong with me...but...but why ya'll coming in here like that? You police now? Is that what it is?"

"Baby, are you using drugs?" Reggie said sternly. "Stop fucking around and tell us right now."

"No...I was just...I was just..."

"Getting high!" He roared. "After you promised me you wouldn't." Reggie walked up to where she stood and slammed his fist into the wall behind her. It crumbled under the weight of his blow. "Why are you doing this to us?"

"Leave me alone!" Tamika yelled running out. "Just leave me alone!"

"Tamika, wait!" I yelled, chasing her.

CHAPTER TWENTY-SEVEN

AMINA

Drillo was seated on a park bench waiting on me. Guilt was apparent in his eyes when I walked up to him. "I'm sorry, Amina." He swallowed. "I'm sorry about...Tamika. I never meant...for her to get involved like I am. I still don't even know how it happened."

"But you did though."

"No! I told her it wasn't a good idea and she said she wanted to know how it would feel to...to..."

"Get high."

"No...to not care." Drillo paused. "She wanted to not care about anything because she said caring and loving hurts too much. And just once she wanted to be...selfish."

I sat next to him. "She wanted to stop caring?"

"Yes." He paused. "But I told her it doesn't help forever. Told her after it wears off she'll be guiltier than she was before doing it. But...but she didn't care."

"Drillo, the damage you did is...is unforgiv—"

"Don't say that."

THE HOUSE THAT CRACK BUILT 2

"I have to."

"Please don't say it, Amina because you won't mean it." He paused. "And you'll feel as guilty as I do right now for turning your brother away in the future. What if I'm ready to change? What if I'm really ready to change?" He paused. "Just...don't give up on me."

"I have tried all I could to bring you back. I put you in rehab eleven times. I chased you around in dope houses and dragged you out by your arms and every time you went in you promised to stay and you didn't. And now look...Tamika is gone under too."

"And I'm so—"

"I can't help you anymore, Drillo." I stood up. "I won't give you anymore money and even if you do go into rehab I won't be there for you."

"What...why?"

"It's obvious already."

"But...but you're my big sister." He said as tears trailed down his face. "You are the only family I have."

"I know and that's why this hurts so badly. I really wanted a happy ending but I'm realizing it will have to wait." I lowered my head. "I love you." I walked away.

"Amina, don't go!" He yelled. "Please!"

When I walked into the house Reggie was on the phone talking to someone and it didn't look good. "What's wrong now?"

He took a deep breath and hung up. "How did things go with Drillo? Everything cool? I know you looked—"

"Reggie!" I yelled. "I know something else is wrong so tell me now. I'm an adult you know."

He nodded. "A friend of mine at the police station says that indictments are coming down and that this house and all of the cars will more than likely be seized. Said we should get ready."

"Seized?" I held my chest. "But...but why...how?"

"I don't have all the details. I was just told to grab everything we can hold and bounce now."

THE HOUSE THAT CRACK BUILT 2

Reggie, April and me were sitting in the living room wondering why we hadn't heard from Russo. I called and texted him a million times and Reggie did the same and we both came up empty-handed. Where was he when we needed him more than ever?

"I don't have a good feeling about this at all." I paused. "He would never not call us after so much time."

"Don't draw conclusions just yet," Reggie said pacing. "He could be out on business right now. Let's just keep a level head because it's not helping things going hysterical."

I looked at April. "Was Naverly sleep?"

"Yeah, but I think she knows something's wrong. Says she doesn't wanna be in grand mommy's house. And that she wanted to go back to daddy's."

I shook my head. "Not even a teenager and already too worried about luxury."

April laughed and I sighed. "She just got used to living there and the food Rosa made." April said. "And that room. Her father used to bring her in little dresses everyday."

I frowned. "What you talking about?"

"He spoiled her rotten," April giggled. "That's why she never wanted to leave. Wait, you didn't know that shit?"

"April, cut it out," Reggie said. "You not helping much at all. You do know that right?"

I was just about to tell her the same thing when I heard glass breaking in the kitchen. Reggie reached for his gun but it wasn't there. "Fuck."

"What's wrong?" I whispered.

"I tossed it after the call. Didn't want the cops catching me holding."

"I'm calling the police," I said, dialing the number before he could change his mind. After giving them the address I grabbed a vodka bottle off the table and stood behind Reggie who released a pocketknife I didn't know he had.

"Ya'll stay behind me." He whispered. "I'm going to see who the fuck that is."

BANG! BANG! BANG!

"It's the police! Open up!" Someone racked on the front door. If that was the cops they got here quick as shit. Normally if you called in the morning it would take until the afternoon.

April quickly opened it and two officers poured inside. "Did someone report a break-in? We were

THE HOUSE THAT CRACK BUILT 2

on the next street over when the call came through."

"Yes," I said walking up to them. "Somebody was trying to get—"

"Found him!" A third officer said walking in the door. He was holding my brother Drillo. "Do you know this person?"

I looked at April and then Reggie. "Yes. But I still want him arrested. He broke into my house."

CHAPTER TWENTY-EIGHT
REGGIE

*R*eggie was mowing the lawn when a cab pulled up in front of the house. The back window rolled down and Gina stuck her head out. "Reggie, can you pay the driver?"

Reggie cut off the mower, dug into his pocket and gave the man one hundred dollars. Way more than what was owed. "Stay right here." He told him. "So you can take her back from wherever she came."

"No problem, man!" He smiled happily.

Gina stepped out of the car and walked over to him. "Reggie, is everything okay?"

He grabbed her by the arm and walked a few feet away from the cab. "You're not welcome here anymore. You're not welcome in my life anymore."

She frowned and took one step back. "What...what did I do?"

"Where do you want me to start?"

"Reggie, if this is about your wife you know how she is!" She said adamantly. "She never liked me no matter what I tried to do. Please don't let her *come in between our relationship. Especially after it took me so long to find you."*

"Took you so long to find me?" He laughed. "I was here the entire time. You never bothered to look because you didn't care. It wasn't until you got up with Peter who wanted revenge on my people that you came back."

"That's not true I—"

"I saw Peter the other day, ma! I know it's true." He paused. *"All I had to do was give him twenty dollars and he gave me every detail."* He shook his head. *"And here it was I thought you were coming back for me and the whole time you had other motives."*

"That's not true, Reggie. Now I will admit, I did let him convince me to come back to get back at your little girlfriend and—"

"Wife!" He yelled. "She's my wife and I'm not gonna let you disrespect her anymore. You done enough damage already."

"So basically you letting her lie on me again!"

"Why do you insist on blaming everybody but yourself? I was a kid when you left! I needed you and you abandoned me. And I hate you for it and I'm allowed to say it. All this time I felt guilty when

I was doing more harm then good. You broke my heart and I'm done."

"Son!"

"Oh, and I know you blocked your house number out just so you could fuck with her head. And guess what it worked. And it's because of you that she's on drugs right now."

Gina's jaw hung. "She's on...drugs?"

"You know what...just forget I even said that." *He ran his hand down his face. "The bottom line is this, you are no longer welcome here. Don't come back. Ever."* *He turned to walk away from her.*

"But, Reggie—"

"Go!" *He yelled louder, pointing at the cab. "Now!"*

"You don't know what I gave up for you." *She paused. "You don't know what I protected you from."*

"I don't know what you're talking about, but I didn't need protection before you came into the picture." *He paused. "Now I'm not gonna say it again."*

She took a deep breath, looked down and walked toward the cab. Once she was inside he walked into the house, slamming the door behind himself.

THE HOUSE THAT CRACK BUILT 2

"April, I need you to promise me that you'll stay in here and look after Tamika," Amina asked. "We shouldn't be that long."

"I already told you that I have you," she said.

"Good," Amina paused. "Me and Reggie are going to look for Russo. I mean, this thing is driving me crazy."

"I understand." April said compassionately. "Go do what you gotta do. I'll be here."

When they left April popped herself some popcorn and sat in the living room. She was about to put on The Planet Of The Apes movie when Tamika walked down the stairs, wrapped in a plaid quilt.

"Everybody finally left?" She asked her cousin.

"Yep. And they have me in here watching a movie by myself. Punks. I'll be good though."

"You mean they have you in here watching me." Tamika flopped next to her and ate a few kernels.

"Why would they do that?" April said playfully. "You're an adult." She shook her head no. "Nah...I just wanted to watch a movie alone. You know how hard it is to get some peace and quiet around here."

"Tell me about it." Tamika looked over at April and then around the house. "Any beer in the fridge? It's better with popcorn."

"Nah...Reggie drank the last one last night."

"Well maybe you can go get a few. I don't know about you but I can definitely do a Corona."

April paused the movie and looked at her. "You're not supposed to be drinking right now...you know...with the drugs and all."

Tamika laughed. "Girl, they really got you in here believing I'm some dope fiend. I used drugs the one time and didn't like it. It got me sick and everything. I'm done with all that shit for real. If they gonna tell you the story it should be the right one."

"I still can't go."

"So you are in here watching me." Tamika frowned. "Because if I didn't know you for anything it was a liar."

"I'm not a liar...I was just...trying to sit back." She shrugged. "Hadn't planned on doing much of anything to be honest. Definitely not going to a liquor store."

"Please." Tamika begged. *"Reggie took the keys to my car and put it somewhere so I can't go myself."* She paused. *"Now are you just Amina's cousin or are you mine too? Because I don't know if you know it or not but I'm the reason she let you back around here. She didn't even trust you when she first saw you."*

April looked at her with wide eyes. Now she had her full attention. *"That's not true."*

"You keep believing that if you want to." She paused. *"I'm the reason you here now are you gonna do something for me or not?"*

"I'll go get the beer."

Tamika hugged her and walked her to the door after she grabbed her purse and keys.

When she left Tamika walked out the back door and hopped over the fence to what used to be Reggie's house. Once there she walked across to the other house across from his and then knocked on the door. A tall young man named Wayne opened it wide. *"Tamika..."* he grinned. *"You back already?"*

"Yes. I need something."

"And I need something too." He opened the door wider and allowed her inside. Next he leaned

against the wall, removed his penis and watched her drop to her knees.

His dick rested on her pink tongue as she satisfied him intensely. She didn't mind, because in a few minutes she would be getting high.

CHAPTER TWENTY-NINE

AMINA

*R*ain poured heavily down on Baltimore City as thunder clapped against the sky overhead. Most of the city's residents chose to stay hidden within the walls of their homes but Amina didn't have the luxury because she was being hunted for dear life by her husband Russo.

"Please leave me alone!" She yelled as she continued to bolt as fast as she could. One of her shoes had fallen off some ways back, which meant her bare toes pressed against broken vials and filth as she dipped in and out of dark alleyways.

But Russo wouldn't give up his chase. Armed with a silver .45 he made it evident that he had one mission, to put his princess out of her misery.

Forever.

When Amina looked back, she tripped over a brick in front of her, causing her to break her big toe. Hysterical, when she rolled on her back, the rain continuing to smack at her face, Russo came into view.

With outstretched hands she begged for her life. "Please don't do this to me. I love you."

He smiled at her sinisterly, cocked his weapon and....BOOM!

Once again I woke up from a terrible dream, one that had taken me hostage every night I went to bed since Russo and I started fighting. Except now I hadn't seen or spoken to him in days. I was just about to try and get some sleep when my bedroom door flew open.

"Amina, they found him." Reggie said.

"Found who?"

"Russo." He said with wide eyes. "We have to go! Now!"

He had been in the hospital for four days and I had no idea. I don't know how I got there but when I did I was almost knocked off my feet when I saw his condition. The thing in the bed didn't look like my husband. His eyes were shut and his face was gaunt and I wondered what took them so long to find me.

Reggie, I guess seeing my frozen state, pushed past me softly to stand at Russo's bedside. Then he extended his hand and said, "It's okay, Amina. He's alive. Come here."

I knew he was telling the truth but at the moment my nerves were bad. But eventually I walked toward the bed, not really looking at him. Instead my eyes fell on Reggie. "I'm sorry I left you at the house."

He smiled. "No need to apologize. I understand." He took a deep breath, looked at Russo and back at me. "Plus if my wife was in here I would've probably split too."

I looked back at the door. "Where is Tamika? Did she come with you?"

"She's at the house."

I sighed. "I hope that's true."

He nodded. "I hope it's true too. But right now I have to find out what's going on with my friend." He looked at Russo. "I'll deal with her later either which way."

"Mrs. Jameson?" The doctor said as he entered the room. "Are you his wife?"

"Yes." I cleared my throat. "I am. Sorry I didn't stop by the office first like you asked. I just really wanted to see him."

"I understand." He looked at Reggie. "And you are?"

"Family." I interjected.

The doctor nodded. "Well I'm afraid I don't have good news. We tried all we could to stop the internal bleeding from the five bullets he sustained to the chest and it hasn't been good. We don't foresee he'll make it through the night."

I dropped to the floor and suddenly I was floating. It took me a few seconds to realize it was Reggie carrying me to the only available recliner in the room.

"Should I come back later?" The doctor asked.

"No." I said almost out of breath. "Please...please continue. I'm, fine. I really am."

"But you look bad."

"She said she's fine." Reggie added. "Just finish what you were saying."

"Okay, well like I said he lost a lot of blood and more than likely he won't make it."

"With all due respect, you don't have the final word." He paused. "God does."

"I think even God would say all is lost in his case."

"On second thought, my man, kick rocks," Reggie said. "'Cause you talking reckless now."

"Okay, I'll be back later."

"Please don't." I said.

THE HOUSE THAT CRACK BUILT 2

The doctor nodded again and walked out.

Reggie shook his head and said, "Don't pay that nigga any attention. You know what you gotta do."

"Yeah. Pray."

Reggie walked over to Russo and touched his arm. "My man, I need you to get up and out this bed. This ain't your story. You got a little girl who needs you. And you got a wife. And..." Reggie couldn't say anymore and was choked up. "I gotta get some air, Amina. I'll be back."

REGGIE

Reggie stepped out in the hall and ran into Tamara. The moment he saw her pretty face he gripped her under her arm an escorted her away from the room and against the wall. "Fuck you doing here? Are you crazy or something?"

I heard he was—"

"Bitch, you gotta bounce."

"But I love him! And I want to—"

"I'm not gonna say it again."

Through flaring nostrils she exhaled deeply. "I'm not gonna stay away from him forever. You do know that right? Nothing will keep us apart. Not even his wife."

"Fuck my nigga do to you that got you batty?"

She looked at her bandaged hand and back at Reggie. She smiled at him and walked away.

THE HOUSE THAT CRACK BUILT 2

CHAPTER THIRTY

TAMIKA

*T*amika sat on the floor while a block hugger paid her fifteen dollars to eat her pussy. As he feasted on her like he hadn't eaten anything ever, she smoked crack from a pipe. Back against the wall, legs wide open she reveled in her high. The man moaned erotically as he rubbed himself on the floor. This was her new life.

She had fallen deeper into the abyss of drugs.

Twenty minutes later, with the john satisfied, she was done and speed walked back to the house. Once there she showered and walked outside where Amina and Reggie were waiting in the car for her to drive with them to pick up Russo. They hadn't seen her come into the house because she entered on the side door.

"Sorry guys." Tamika said as she slid into the backseat. "Was enjoying my shower."

"Don't worry about that, bae," Reggie said. "It's a good day."

"Right!" Amina added from the passenger seat.

As they continued to drive, Tamika noticed they were going the opposite way. All she could do was shake her head when she realized what was happening. Now that she thought about it earlier she noticed Amina and Reggie giving each other knowing glances and now everything made sense.

"Wow." Tamika said.

"What, bae?" Reggie said staring at her from the rear view mirror.

"I know, Reggie."

He looked at Amina who turned around to focus on her sister. "I'm sorry, Tamika. I really am. I wish there was some other way but unfortunately we've come to this."

Tamika took a deep breath. "Don't be sorry. I knew this would happen and I understand. At least ya'll love me enough to bring me here."

"I'm glad because we couldn't think of any other way to help you. And we need you back to yourself."

Tamika was taking it on the chin but like most addicts she started to realize that help meant she would know longer have the sensation that she did when things got rough. She wouldn't be able to depend on drugs anymore for her temporary relief when she missed her mom, brother or tried to shake the feelings of hate she had for Reggie allowing his mother to enter their lives.

THE HOUSE THAT CRACK BUILT 2

Basically rehab meant she would be forced to deal with all of her problems, including the rape while she was clean and she wasn't ready for what that would feel like.

"Look...I thought about it...I don't wanna go right now. I'll go next month." She sat in the middle of the backseat and scooted up so she could look at them. "I'll get better on my own, I promise."

"Sorry, Tamika. But we can't do that. Trust me, this will be good." Reggie said. "That way we can go back to the way things used to be."

He was talking crazy in her opinion now. Tamika looked at the doors and contemplated how much it would hurt if she jumped out and rolled into the street.

"What about Russo?" Tamika asked. "I wanted to be here when he came back."

"You'll be better when you see him." Reggie said. "At your best."

They made it to rehab and Tamika sobbed uncontrollably as she tried to barter with them. I won't leave the house. I won't drink. I'll do whatever just please don't leave me here. She even tried to take off but Reggie was able to overcome her and as her husband, who was acting as her guardian, he was able to check her in.

Amina was right; Russo was alive and did survive. But if you'd hear him tell it being in the wheelchair was just like death because he was told he would never walk again.

That was the last of the bad news. Because he lost it all in his opinion. His house, his cars, his ability to walk and he was even facing a king pin charge. So when his wife carried on like all would be okay because she prayed on it, it drove him up a wall.

As Reggie and Amina wheeled him into the house that crack built, he couldn't help but plot his come back despite the obstacles.

And he had plans to be as vicious as ever.

"Are you hungry?" Amina asked Russo. "I was going to make a tuna sandwich."

"A beer or something too, man?" Reggie asked him also.

"He can't drink a beer right now," Amina joked. "He's—"

THE HOUSE THAT CRACK BUILT 2

"I can drink whatever I want," Russo said, putting her in place. "Now both of you just leave me alone. I got a lot of shit on my mind."

Amina looked at him and took off running upstairs. Reggie followed her. "Just give him time."

"You don't understand, this is all my fault," she wept, throwing herself onto her bed. "All my fucking fault. If I hadn't met him he would still be walking."

"How you gonna blame yourself? The Black Nazi been after Russo ever since he took over his D.C. territory."

Amina slowly looked up at him. "This…is…because of a situation he had before he met me? Before we moved into this house?"

"Yeah, what did you think it was about?"

Amina's heart thumped wildly in her chest. Russo told her his predicament was about the house and now she learned that once again he lied. Slowly she stood up and moved toward the bathroom.

"Amina," Reggie said softly. "Are you okay?"

She closed the door and he continued to call her name.

"Amina…"

She placed her hands on the sink and looked at her reflection in the mirror. Russo was both loving and hateful and she was finding this out as her marriage continued with him. All of the lies, all of the drama was to do one thing and one thing only, his desire to get her to move out of the very house he hated so much and now had to live in because his was gone.

Was she going to leave him?

Not even close.

But what she was going to do was make his life a living hell in a wheelchair.

Her good girl routine was out the window. And was replaced with something else.

"Sorry, mama. But you won't like me after this."

THE HOUSE THAT CRACK
BUILT 3
TAMIKA & REGGIE

COMING SOON!

THE HOUSE THAT CRACK BUILT 2

The Cartel Publications Order Form

www.thecartelpublications.com

Inmates **ONLY** receive novels for $10.00 per book.

(Mail Order **MUST** come from inmate directly to receive discount)

Shyt List 1	_____	$15.00
Shyt List 2	_____	$15.00
Shyt List 3	_____	$15.00
Shyt List 4	_____	$15.00
Shyt List 5	_____	$15.00
Pitbulls In A Skirt	_____	$15.00
Pitbulls In A Skirt 2	_____	$15.00
Pitbulls In A Skirt 3	_____	$15.00
Pitbulls In A Skirt 4	_____	$15.00
Pitbulls In A Skirt 5	_____	$15.00
Victoria's Secret	_____	$15.00
Poison 1	_____	$15.00
Poison 2	_____	$15.00
Hell Razor Honeys	_____	$15.00
Hell Razor Honeys 2	_____	$15.00
A Hustler's Son	_____	$15.00
A Hustler's Son 2	_____	$15.00
Black and Ugly	_____	$15.00
Black and Ugly As Ever	_____	$15.00
Year Of The Crackmom	_____	$15.00
Deadheads	_____	$15.00
The Face That Launched A	_____	$15.00
Thousand Bullets		
The Unusual Suspects	_____	$15.00
Miss Wayne & The Queens of DC	_____	$15.00
Paid In Blood (eBook Only)	_____	$15.00
Raunchy	_____	$15.00
Raunchy 2	_____	$15.00
Raunchy 3	_____	$15.00
Mad Maxxx	_____	$15.00
Quita's Dayscare Center	_____	$15.00
Quita's Dayscare Center 2	_____	$15.00
Pretty Kings	_____	$15.00
Pretty Kings 2	_____	$15.00
Pretty Kings 3	_____	$15.00
Pretty Kings 4	_____	$15.00
Silence Of The Nine	_____	$15.00
Silence Of The Nine 2	_____	$15.00
Prison Throne	_____	$15.00
Drunk & Hot Girls	_____	$15.00
Hersband Material	_____	$15.00
The End: How To Write A	_____	$15.00
Bestselling Novel In 30 Days (Non-Fiction Guide)		
Upscale Kittens	_____	$15.00
Wake & Bake Boys	_____	$15.00
Young & Dumb	_____	$15.00
Young & Dumb 2:	_____	$15.00
Tranny 911	_____	$15.00
Tranny 911: Dixie's Rise	_____	$15.00

First Comes Love, Then Comes Murder _____	$15.00
Luxury Tax _____	$15.00
The Lying King _____	$15.00
Crazy Kind Of Love _____	$15.00
And They Call Me God _____	$15.00
The Ungrateful Bastards _____	$15.00
Lipstick Dom _____	$15.00
A School of Dolls _____	$15.00
Hoetic Justice _____	$15.00
KALI: Raunchy Relived _____	$15.00
Skeezers _____	$15.00
You Kissed Me, Now I Own You _____	$15.00
Nefarious _____	$15.00
Redbone 3: The Rise of The Fold _____	$15.00
The Fold _____	$15.00
Clown Niggas _____	$15.00
The One You Shouldn't Trust _____	$15.00
The WHORE The Wind	
Blew My Way _____	$15.00
She Brings The Worst Kind _____	$15.00
The House That Crack Built _____	$15.00
The House That Crack Built _____	$15.00

(**Redbone 1 & 2** are **NOT** Cartel Publications novels and if **ordered** the cost is **FULL** price of $15.00 **each. No Exceptions**.)

Please add $5.00 **PER BOOK** for shipping and handling.

The Cartel Publications * P.O. BOX 486 OWINGS MILLS MD 21117

Name: _____

Address: _____

City/State: _____

Contact/Email: _____

Please allow 5-7 BUSINESS days before shipping.

The Cartel Publications is NOT responsible for Prison Orders rejected, NO RETURNS and NO REFUNDS.

NO PERSONAL CHECKS ACCEPTED

STAMPS NO LONGER ACCEPTED

THE HOUSE THAT CRACK BUILT 2

www.ingramcontent.com/pod-product-compliance
Lightning Source LLC
Chambersburg PA
CBHW022007050726
47499CB00003BA/713